Love, Lust, & Infatuation

Kandis & Kayla Issac

Chapter 1: Imagine

Celeste Norwood

Been through some bad shit, I should be a sad bitch
Who woulda thought it'd turn me to a savage?
Rather be tied up with calls and not strings
~Ariana Grande

"Babe? How do I look?" I asked, coming out of my walk-in closet, dressed in my red Versace Medusa accent knitted dress, with a pair of gold Versace Medusa sandal heels. My natural curly 4C hair was braided down under my twenty-eight inches of Brazilian body wave bundles. My makeup looked as if God himself slayed it, and I was feeling rejuvenated after the spa day I had the day before with my sister.

Doing a spin, I smiled from ear-to-ear, waiting for my husband to acknowledge me. When I noticed his head was still buried into his MacBook Pro, I sighed and shook my head.

"Kadarius!" I yelled, snapping my fingers in his face.

"What, baby? I'm working."

"Can you please get your face out of that damn laptop for two seconds? It's like I have to tell you this a thousand times every day."

Kadarius sighed and placed his laptop to the side before looking at me with his arms crossed. He knew that I wanted his attention, and his reaction wasn't something that I was expecting because he looked up at me as if I was bothering him.

"What is it?" he asked, still with the same stale face expression.

"You know what, fuck it. Go back to your work if I'm bothering you," I replied, rolling my eyes, and walking back off into my closet to grab my purse.

When I walked out of my closet, he was stepping in. I rolled my eyes, seeing him close the door and walk over to me, placing his hands on my back, pulling me close.

"I'm sorry baby, I've just been so booked with all these new cases."

"Okay and, whenever I get booked with writing, I always try to make time for my family. I hate that we have to have this conversation every day of the week."

"I'm sorry."

"Keep your sorry. I'm about to head out."

"Where are you going looking all fine and shit?"

"I'm going out to my sister's bookstore to sign copies of my book and meet my supporters."

"Dressed like that?"

"First impressions are everything, Kadarius. Besides, as soon as I leave there, my sister and I are having brunch with my mother later."

"She's coming here?"

"Yeah, she's only here for a few days."

"That's good. I can't remember the last time I saw your mama."

"That makes both of us. When are you going to come to one of my book signings? I can't remember the last time you came to one. Let's talk about that."

"How about we don't." He smirked, planting a kiss on my lips.

"Bye, I gotta go. The least you can do is take the twins to their doctor's appointment."

"I got you," he replied, leaning in to kiss me.

I poked my lips out and frowned when he kissed my cheek, thinking he was aiming for my lips. I decided not to say anything about it because I knew I wasn't going to get anywhere with him. Turning on my heels, I walked out of my closet and gave Kadarius one last glance. He was still on that damn laptop.

Walking out of the bedroom, I made my way downstairs to see my six-year-old twins Cassie and Kadarius Junior in the kitchen eating cereal with their eyes glued to the TV, watching *The Adventures of SharkBoy and LavaGirl*. I decided on simply making my way out because I knew if I stopped, they would beg me to go, and the last thing I needed was to keep an eye on them, sign books, and greet people. I made my way over to my all-white Rolls Royce, and got in, making my way to my sister Charlotte's bookstore.

"Imagine" by Ariana Grande blasted through the speakers of my car as I made a stop by Starbucks to get my usual white chocolate creme frappe, with caramel drizzle and a blueberry muffin. Deciding to park on the side where the employee's parked, I got out and went inside through the side door to avoid the massive crowd that was piled at the front of the store. When I came to the front, there stood my big sister Charlotte pulling copies of my new book from boxes.

"Hey, big sis," I greeted, walking over with open arms.

Charlotte placed the books on the table before turning around, looking at me with an enormous smile on her face. She pulled me into a hug, rocking me from side to side.

"Well, if it isn't the woman of the hour. Got those people out there waiting on you. They act like you, Beyoncé."

"What's wrong? Being Kelly and Michelle is too much for you?" I laughed.

"You think you funny, huh? I would consider myself La-toya."

"Oh, god, whatever."

"I'm for real, but most of them have been hanging outside since six a.m."

"What can I say, I can write my ass off," I replied, flipping my hair and picking up my bestselling book, *Fire, Ice, and Chains.*

"You got that right. I've been up since three in the morning reading your book, *Dipped in Gold.* Bitch, you must be a secret porn star because I've never in my life read any kind of the freaky shit like that before."

"I'm just a very imaginative person, but hey, I will need some extra hands in the next two weeks."

"With what?"

"I have this huge meet and greet in Seattle. This event will be the biggest event of my life. I'm going to not only be launching my new book, but I have some big news as well that all my supporters will love."

"Seattle, huh?"

"Yes, are you down?"

"You know I'm down. I'm so proud of you." Charlotte smiled, pulling me into another hug.

"It took a lot to get where I am. I'm proud of myself too, and I wouldn't have even gotten this far without my wonderful team."

"Aw, ok, enough of the sappy shit, I'm about to let your fans in."

"Okay, I'm ready," I replied, taking a seat behind the table that was piled up with copies of my books and merchandise with my name on it.

As soon as I heard that bell, people began lining up, bringing a Cheshire cat smile on my face.

"Oh my god, it's really you, C.K Norwood?" a girl exclaimed, clenching a copy of one of my books to her chest.

"Yes, it is. Hi, nice to meet you, sweetheart."

"Wow, I came all the way from Georgia to see you, I've been reading your books since DreamPen days."

"Oh my god, that was so long ago. I miss those days. I'm thinking about going back to DreamPen. Thank you so much for being a day one supporter."

"No, thank you for writing such amazing content," she replied, passing me her book. I took it and grabbed my pink gel pen, signing my name in it.

"What's your name, doll?"

"Janice."

"To Janice, with love C.K Norwood." I smiled.

"Thank you so much."

"No problem," I replied, passing her the book back, and she left the line.

"C.K Norwood, I remember back on DreamPen, your username was TheBestofCeleste." Looking up from the table, I brought my attention to the man who looked at me with nothing but desire in his eyes.

Chapter 2: Star Struck

Raymon Stevens

All I gotta say is that I must be dreaming, can't be real
You're not here with me, still I can feel you near me
~Michael Jackson

After what seemed like an eternity, I was finally gazing into the eyes of the infamous C.K. Norwood. I had been reading her work since her DreamPen days. When I first read her writing, I thought she was a man, but after researching her on social media, I found out she was a woman. A beautiful woman, might I add. After looking at her pictures, I would often fantasize about her while reading her books. I would picture putting her in the sexual positions that she would write about. Though I had to admit it, I would often jack off to her pictures. To some, it might have sounded weird, but I didn't care.

"C.K Norwood, I remember back on DreamPen, your username was TheBestofCeleste."

"I haven't been on DreamPen in forever. I've been meaning to go back. I appreciate you following my career, Mr...?"

"Stevens...Raymon Stevens. It's a pleasure to finally meet you. Your books are amazing," I flirted.

"Thank you, Raymon. Let me sign this for you."

She signed my book and handed it to me. When she did, our hands touched, and I felt a bolt of electricity shoot through my body. Looking into her eyes, I could tell she felt it too.

"Thank you, Mrs. Norwood."

"No, thank you for your support, and please call me Celeste."

"Ok, Celeste. Listen, I don't want to hold you up, but I was wondering if you would be interested in doing a book discussion. I am the head of a group, and we discuss a different book twice a month."

"I would love to. Here's my card. Please e-mail me the details."

I took her card, making sure that I brushed against her hand once more. That same bolt that I felt before went through me again. This time it caused Celeste to jump. I winked at her before walking away.

Rather than leave the bookstore, I stood at a distance and watched her. She greeted each reader with a warm smile, some got hugs, and some took pictures with her. I wanted to slap myself for not thinking to ask for a hug. There would be other times for that, though. Instead, I pulled out my phone, zoomed the camera in as close as I could, and snapped a few pictures of her. I moved across the room as much as I could without being noticed to get images from different angles.

After about an hour of watching her, I headed home so that I could reach out to my book club about the discussion. I was president of a club called Book Lovers Anonymous. We got together twice a month to discuss a book. We also traveled to various book events to meet the authors we loved to read.

Having an author attend one of our book discussions was something we always wanted to do but had yet to accomplish. Luckily, we hadn't chosen a book for our next read yet. Hell, even if we had, as president, I could always change it.

When I got home, I sent out a group text, letting everyone know that Celeste had agreed to attend the discussion. Most of them wrote back immediately, letting me know how excited they were about the discussion. It was decided that we would be discussing her latest release, *Fire, Ice, and Chains.* Most of us had already read the book, so we simply had to wait for the date.

Once everything was confirmed, I e-mailed Celeste the date, time, and location of the discussion. After I sent the e-mail, I pulled out my phone to look at the pictures I had taken of her earlier. While looking at them, I imagined what it would be like to have her full brown lips pushed against mine. Looking at them, I could tell they were soft.

My mind wandered a little further, and I imagined them on my dick, which caused me to get hard. Not being able to fight the urge, I pulled out my dick and started stroking it while moaning her name. I didn't care what it took, Celeste Norwood would be mine.

Chapter 3: When Dedication is Her Key

Celeste

After signing books and conversing with all of my supporters for three hours straight, I found myself at Bocelli's, in Staten Island, with my mother and two sisters, enjoying lunch. Since my mother was in town for a while, I found every possible moment I could have with her. My mother was like my rock when it came to everything in life. I was the baby out of all five of my siblings, and I was the closest to both of my parents than any of them. My mother was my biggest supporter since I began writing, and when I say she was feeding me dedication like a five-course meal, she was doing just that.

My mother, Jackie, was my backbone, and she was the one who pushed me to go full-on public with my work. If it weren't for her, I would still be stuck settling for less, writing on Dream-Pen with thousands or millions of followers.

"You look so lovely today, sweetheart," my mother complimented.

"Thank you, mama. You do too."

"So, how was the book signing?"

"It was amazing, I haven't had a book signing in a while, and I forgot how amazing it was to be surrounded by people who enjoy my work. It's like seeing them, and hearing them, motivates me to push myself harder."

"You got that right. I've never seen so many people in my store at once. I knew my baby sister was big, but I didn't know she was that big. Girl, we might have to get you your own show soon," Charlotte commented.

"I'm getting there. I just can't wait for this big event I have planned in Seattle. I can't wait share the big news with everyone here today. It's something that I've wanted for so long."

"Please don't tell me you pregnant. As busy as Kadarius and you both are when do the both of you have time to make a baby?" Angela, my big sister, added.

"Oh God no, the twins are already enough by their lonesome. And you're right about one thing. I'm the least of Kadarius' worries right now. That man is more dedicated to being a lawyer than being a husband sometimes." I sighed, taking a sip of my Chardonnay.

"Sweetie, everyone has to work. You're a full-time author, and you're getting popular by the day. You're so huge that you have bodyguards following you around at every event you go to. That man is just getting his first law firm, so of course, he will be busy. Both of you work to make a life for those babies at home. Just remember all that work will pay off, and both of you will have time to go back to how things used to be," my mother encouraged, cutting into her steak.

"I know, mama."

"Good, so tell me about this big news you have us all sitting on ice for."

"I'm keeping this news to myself until my event, mama."

"Well, you have me anxious."

"I know, but trust me, the wait will be worth it."

"I hope so," Angela said, taking a fork full of garlic mashed potatoes and stuffing her mouth.

We all conversed about my career, along with my preparations for my event in Seattle. Once we finished with lunch, we all went our separate ways. Due to the twins being out of school for today, I knew the house would be noisy, so I decided to do some work at a nearby cafe on the way home.

Parallel parking on the side, I grabbed my pink MacBook Pro and made my way inside.

Buying a bottle of water, I took a seat near the window and opened my MacBook. Entering my password, I opened the document to the second part of my book, *Fire, Ice, and Chains*. I decided on doing a second part due to how much attention I was getting on book one. *Fire, Ice, and Chains* was so hot that I was even recognized on TV for having such a spicy suspenseful novel.

When my name was said on TV by the most popular television host out there, I almost pulled my wig off and did flips. I had big things coming my way from left and right and I couldn't do anything but thank God for getting me this far. As soon as I was about to start typing, I received an e-mail popping up at the right corner of my laptop screen. Clicking the e-mail, I licked my lips and read it in my head.

From: Raymon Stevens

To: Author C.K Norwood

Wow, I can't believe I'm actually e-mailing the one and only Celeste Norwood. I don't know if you remember me from the book signing, but I'm the guy who asked if you could attend one of my book discussions. I'm a huge fan of your work, and it was such an honor to see you in person. You're indeed a beautiful woman and you knew how to light up a room today. I hope 2:30 p.m. this Saturday in Manhattan is okay. I live in Lenox Hill, apartment 3B. We can't wait to discuss your novel Fire, Ice, and Chains. See you then, Celeste.

Replying quickly to his e-mail, I agreed on the timing. I couldn't remember the last time I've attended a book discussion, one discussing my work at that. Raising my eyebrow in curiosity, I clicked his e-mail profile picture and stared at it like it was a prize. This man was indeed something pleasant for the eyes. I was so busy trying to get to everyone at the book signing that I didn't get a good glance at him. It was something about him that made me feel some type of way. It was like the energy he was giving off sent chills down my spine.

His profile photo was a picture of him at the beach, coming out of the water. The sun was reflecting off his built chiseled body, as his tattoos covered his light skin chest like paint on a once blank canvas. Water dripped from his beard like a faucet, and his smile was as big as the ocean.

I clenched my legs together, feeling the waterfall forming in my white laced Victoria Secret panties. I shook those thoughts quickly from my head and unscrewed the cap from my Aquafina water, taking it to the head like it was liquor. I couldn't remember the last time my husband touched me, and it was indeed sad. It was as if my rabbit vibrator gave me more attention than my man did, and it was a disgrace. Kadarius made me feel as if something was wrong with me, and he wasn't attracted to me anymore. I even tried to please him, and he would push me away.

Most of the time, I just wish I could switch lives with the characters that I wrote about. I wanted to be bent over the ledge of the balcony of an expensive hotel, being fucked like a porn star, sipping on the most exotic wines. I wanted my man to devour my pussy like it was the last supper. I wanted to be touched and caressed, but I was getting no play. It was so bad to where I would force myself to dream about being in my character's positions. Shit, I barely had time to please myself because my kids were like two parrots, always in my ear. The only time I could be alone was when Kadarius left me early in the morning to go to work and while the kids were off to school.

Picking up my phone, I decided on texting my best friend

Jolani to see if she felt like going out to a club sometime next week. I needed to find some type of fun in my life because I felt as if all I did was write, take care of my kids, and be a wife to my husband.

The last time I went to a club was when Kadarius and I conceived the twins in the back of his dad's blue Cadillac convertible. I remember when we would do exciting shit like that, spontaneous stuff that gave me a rush. Now all his dedication was toward work, just work. My dedication was toward my job, my kids, and to him, but he didn't notice. Kadarius wouldn't notice me if I were standing right in front of him.

I shook my head in disgust at how sad my life seemed right now. I may have had it all with my writing career kicking off, but things at home were horrendous. Instead of letting all these feelings eat me up inside, I began typing away. The sound of my all white stiletto acrylic nails tapped away at the keys of my MacBook.

"Chapter one, where her needs aren't fulfilled," I thought aloud, typing.

Chapter 4: Hiding in Plain Sight

What you say to me I can't hear a thing
Try to talk some sense to myself, but I won't listen
I'm what God made of me
No need to pretend
~Kali Uchis

"Mr. Norwood, there is a Reginald Blake here to see you," my secretary announced.

What the fuck is he doing here? I asked myself before telling her to send him to my office. Reginald knew better than to just pop up at my office unannounced. He was being real reckless right now. We had an agreement and popping up at my office wasn't part of it.

Knock...knock...knock!

"Come in!" I angrily yelled.

"Hey. How are you today?" Reginald greeted me when he came in the door.

"What the hell are you doing here, Reggie?"

"You haven't been answering my calls, so I had to make sure you were okay."

"We just saw each other three days ago!"

"And you haven't answered my calls since. Have I done something wrong?"

Reggie and I met about a year ago at a convention at the Stratosphere Hotel in Las Vegas. He is a law clerk at another firm in New York. I noticed him as soon as I walked into the room, I couldn't help but notice how handsome he was. His jet-black hair was full of waves and went well with his mocha-colored skin. His facial hair was minimal, which was a plus for me. We both stood about six feet tall. I heard one of his colleagues say his name when they were greeting him.

Throughout our meetings, I kept stealing glances at Reggie. I was trying to tell from his mannerisms if he was into men or not, but soon realized I couldn't. Hell, you couldn't tell from looking at me that I messed with men from time to time.

Once all the meetings were over for the day, I headed to the bar that was in the casino. As I was about to place my order, I heard a voice beside me say:

"I'll have a Hennessy and Coke on the rocks. Oh, and please give this gentleman whatever he would like."

While the bartender was making our drinks, he introduced himself, we started drinking together, and about an hour later we were in my room in the sixty-nine-position giving each other some amazing oral pleasure.

From that day forward, we had been inseparable. I found myself wanting to be with Reggie more than I did Celeste. It wasn't I didn't love her, he and I just had more in common. We went to sporting events, bars, and sexed each other crazy. Even though it was wrong, I had completely stopped having sex with my wife.

Things were perfect between us until about six months ago. Reggie started wanting more and more of my attention. I was already in hot water at home and didn't want to make it worse. Reggie was a fling for me that I knew would eventually get old. Celeste was my wife and the mother of my children. I wouldn't dare leave her for another man. Reggie wasn't trying to hear that shit, though.

"Kadarius? Are you listening to me?"

"My bad, what did you say?"

"I asked when you would stop treating me like I'm a side piece?"

"News flash! You are a side piece. In case you forgot, I'm married."

"I don't hear shit about you being married when your dick is down my throat."

He had a point, but I would never tell him that. We started arguing back and forth. Reggie begged and pleaded for me to stop ignoring him. He wanted things to go back to the way they used to be between us.

As I was about to tell him no, Celeste sent me a text ranting about how she hoped I made it home in time for dinner for once. She also said some shit about my kids were starting to forget what I looked like. Not wanting to deal with her bullshit, I told my secretary I was leaving for the day and followed Reggie to the loft we owned in Manhattan. I planned to eventually break things off with him, but today wasn't the day.

Chapter 5: Where She Is Stuck In My Mind

Raymon

I can't get enough of you
Shawty show me what's up with you
There's lots of things that I want to do
But tell me what you can do
'Cause I know there's things that he didn't show you
Let me be your teacher while up in the bedroom
~Roy Woods

"I've never done anything like this," the girl I brought home stated.

We were in my blue room, the room I designed personally after reading C.K Norwood's book *Fire, Ice, and Chains*. I was always a dominant, aggressive man when it came to being in the bedroom, but after reading her work, my sexual desires and fantasies were growing stronger. Shit, after seeing how beautiful she was in person, my desires grew like a forest fire. I've been trying to find a woman strong enough to handle me in the bedroom and try the shit that I'm into, the shit Celeste wrote about.

"I don't like a woman who teases. I told you I'm a man of plenty of secrets," I replied, walking around her, admiring her body as if it was a fresh T-Bone steak that was sitting on the grill. This girl was nowhere close to Celeste Norwood, but she had to do. Since I couldn't have the real thing, I might as well settle for what I had — *for now*.

"Oh, I don't tease, I like to get down to business." She smirked, grabbing my shirt, and pulling me toward the bed.

I grabbed her by her waist and looked down, smirking, imaging her naked. It was as if those thoughts were being spoken aloud, because she pulled her straps from her dress down, and pulled it down, leaving her in nothing but her white lingerie. Her white lingerie complimented her dark skin tone as the fluorescent blue lights bounced off of her skin like the sun bouncing off of a mirror. Taking my shirt off, I threw it to the side, pulling a gold Magnum from my wallet and dropping my True Religion jeans.

She pulled my Tommy Hilfiger boxers down, biting her lips with lust-filled eyes. I tore the Magnum wrapper open with my teeth and placed it over my already hard dick.

"Show me that aggressive shit you were talking about in the club." She smirked, grabbing my balls, and kissing on my tattoos.

I bit my lips, getting turned on by how sexy she was looking right now. I grabbed her by her neck roughly, catching her off guard, pushing her down onto the black silk sheets. I ripped her panties from her body before forcing her legs open.

"Can you slow down?" she asked, placing her hands on top of mine, which was still wrapped around her neck.

Ignoring her, I placed my dick at her entrance, ramming myself in her, ignoring her scream. It was as if my body went into hyper drive when her tight, wet walls gripped around me. I began sending hard thrust into her body, tightening my grip around her neck.

"Fuck!" I groaned, looking up to the ceiling, penetrating her body with all the strength I had in me.

I closed my eyes, imaging that the woman that I was inside of was Celeste. The vision in my head of Celeste's breasts bouncing around as I fucked her hard like it was a sport stuck to my head like glue.

"Damn, right there, Celeste!" I groaned aloud, still with

my eyes closed.

Once I bust my nut, I opened my eyes and looked down to see the girl, unconscious. I didn't even notice I was still choking her. Pulling out, I tossed my condom in the trash can, before grabbing a bottle of water from the side and pouring it on her face. As soon as the water went into her nose, her body jolted up, and she started crying and screaming.

"Shut the fuck up, for somebody into aggressive shit, you blacked out quick," I ranted while putting my boxers back on.

"You're fucking crazy! You almost killed me! I was telling you to stop!" she yelled, crying, trying to rush and put her clothes back on.

"Be bout that action next time, sweetheart. You know where the door is." I replied, getting a cigarette from my nightstand, and lighting it.

"I'm calling the fucking cops."

"And telling them what? You picked up a random dude at the club and let him fuck you?" I laughed to myself.

"You fucking raped me!"

"I did no such thing. I did exactly what you wanted me to do. You gave me permission to do whatever the hell I wanted to do to you, so I took that."

"You're going to fucking jail! And whoever Celeste is, I hope she knows how fucking psychotic you are!"

I walked over to her, backing her up into a wall, watching fear burst through her body like electricity.

"This is what you're gonna do, sweetheart. You're gonna keep her fucking name out of your mouth for number one. And foremost, if you call the cops on me, I'm gonna make your life a living hell, you hear me?"

She remained silent, which made me even angrier. I knelt and grabbed her wallet, pulling her license out.

"Samantha Klein, age twenty-three, height five foot four, you're a Pisces, and you live in East Harlem. I would hate to have to make a trip to East Harlem and pay you a lil visit," I voiced, watching her turn white. I blew my cigarette smoke in her face, waiting for an answer.

"Okay, okay, just let me go, and I won't say a word to anyone."

"I know you wouldn't. Have a nice night, Samantha," I replied, pecking her lips, and watching her run away.

Once I heard my front door close, I got back in my bed, pulling my phone out, going to Celeste's photos that I took of her. I licked my lips, suddenly growing hard again just from looking at her. Her beautiful smile, caramel skin tone, the way her eyes brighten up when she smiled, how soft and strong her legs looked in that dress. I just wondered how tight she would be able to wrap those beautiful brown legs around my head.

I reached into my boxers and closed my eyes, taking myself into deep thoughts about her. I couldn't wait to have her here in front of me during my book discussion. I couldn't wait to be in the same room with her. I couldn't do anything but count down those days, and it was killing me softly.

Chapter 6: My Man

*Oh, you let me down
I am so confused
Stood right by your side through everything
that you went through
~Tamar Braxton*

I sat at my kitchen table, watching my kids eat their dinner and talk about their day at school. My eyes then wandered off to Kadarius' seat at the head of the table which was empty.

"Mama, where's daddy?" my daughter, Cassie asked.

"He's still at work." I sighed, pushing my spaghetti around on my glass plate.

"But it's 8:30," KJ noted.

"I know, maybe he got stuck in traffic. He'll be home soon."

"But he was supposed to help me with my science project." KJ pouted.

"I can help you, baby. Daddy has just been busy at work."

"If you say so." Cassie frowned.

"I know so, how about this? How about next week, I take both of you to Six Flags?" I smiled, hoping it would brighten up their mood. They just sat there with blank faces, not even excited about that. It was as if bribing them with trips and gifts were getting old to them because they genuinely missed their father, I missed him.

"Can I excuse myself, please?" Cassie asked.

"Sure, clean up your mess."

"Can I go too, mama?" KJ asked with the same disappointed look on his face.

I shook my head as they both placed their leftovers in the fridge and went upstairs to their bedroom. All I did was sigh and look across the table at Kadarius' empty spot. I tried to find it in me not to cry because of him missing dinner with his kids. It was something that was becoming a habit. It seemed as if I was texting and calling a phone that was disconnected. Kadarius left me on read and declined my call like I was the IRS.

Getting up, I threw away my untouched food and cleaned the kitchen. Looking down at Kadarius' plate, I threw his food away and slammed the dish in the sink, watching it break. I didn't even notice a tear escape my eyes until it hit my hand. I was crying because it truly hurt me that my man was out there, ignoring me. It was as if everything between us was going south. He rarely talked to me, he didn't touch me, and he did nothing with me. It hurt me that even at night, he didn't hold me like he used to.

I was coming to think that he was sneaking around on me, but I wanted to give my man the benefit of the doubt. Kadarius would never hurt me like that, he would never cheat on me, not my man.

Biting my lip, I sniffled and wiped my eyes with my wrist, since my hands were wet from doing dishes. After drying my hands, I made my way upstairs to take a shower. While passing both of the twins' bedrooms, I noticed that both doors were closed. The twins were more attached to Kadarius since they came out of the womb. Kadarius was the parent who let them get away with everything and who babied them when I was less lenient. Kadarius wasn't only ignoring me, but he was pushing his kids away as well. It was getting to where they had to catch the bus home, or I would have to drop them off and pick them up because Kadarius would be too busy.

Kadarius was supposed to be home at 6:30 today, and I

even checked in with his receptionist to know for sure the time he was coming home. It was going on nine o'clock, and this man was nowhere in sight.

Walking into my bathroom that was adjoined to my bedroom, I stripped out of my clothes and took a quick shower. For a moment, I just stared up at the showerhead with my eyes closed, letting the water run down my face like rain.

"Fuck!" I yelled to myself, taking a deep breath.

Running my hands down my face, trying to get the excess water off, I turned off the faucet, shutting off the water. Getting out of the shower, I dried off and threw on a pair of Kadarius' old basketball shorts and a tank top. After putting on a pair of mix-matched socks, I threw on my cheetah print bonnet and headed toward the twin's bedroom to check on them.

Opening Cassie's door, she was fast asleep with her music playing low in the background. Turning to KJ's room, he was fast asleep on his floor in front of his half-done science project that he started. Smiling, I walked in and picked him up, placing him in bed. He was only six, and he was growing like grass in spring. Once I laid him down in bed, I pulled his Naruto covers over him and kissed his cheek.

"I love you so much, KJ." I smiled, caressing his cheek.

All I could do was think back to the day I gave birth to him and his sister. KJ was the spitting image of Kadarius, and you would think someone hit the copy and paste button. He had Kadarius' same light skin complexion, deep dimples, and he even had Kadarius doing his hair the exact same way as his.

Looking into my son's eyes tonight explaining why his father wasn't present hurt me to the core because I truly didn't have an answer for him. Turning the light off in his bedroom, I walked downstairs to the kitchen and made my way to the cabinets.

I stood on my tiptoes because my five foot three and a

half frame wouldn't reach the top cabinet without me doing so. I grabbed a wine glass from the top shelf and went to my secret stash, grabbing a bottle of Cabernet Sauvignon. Popping the cork off of the wine glass, I poured it in my glass until it reached the rim. I hopped on top of my marble island top and stared at the front door, waiting for my man to bust through the door, hoping and praying he would.

I took the glass to the head before placing it near me. Grabbing my iPhone 11 Pro, I went to Kadarius' contact and tried FaceTiming him for what seemed like the hundredth time. It didn't even ring. It just declined like that. I wanted to throw my phone across the room because I was getting worried by the minute.

It was as if hours went by, and he still wasn't home. It was two o'clock in the morning, and I found myself watching old videos of Kadarius and me at our wedding.

"Wassup everybody, I finally made the woman of my dreams, Mrs. Norwood," Kadarius voiced, planting a kiss on my cheek.

"I love you so much." I smiled, taking my veil off.

"I love you more, beautiful. I'll always love you, I'll always be by your side, and I'll always make you happy."

"I'm so lucky."

"Give me a kiss with your lucky ass." He laughed, grabbing my chin, pulling me in for a kiss.

I cried silently, looking at how happy I was in that moment. All the shit he told me was slowly fading away.

Exiting out of my camera roll, I twisted my engagement ring around my finger, debating on if I wanted to take it off. I didn't even feel like a married woman. I just felt like a single mother with a roommate. Hopping off of the island, I walked upstairs to my bedroom and locked the door, giving Kadarius a hint to sleep on the couch. Going to my walk-in closet, I pulled my rabbit vibrator from my shoebox and went to my bed, pulling my panties to the side and switching the vibrator on.

As soon as I placed the rabbit at my entrance, I threw my head back, biting my lip. After pleasuring myself, I found myself still wide awake at four in the morning. Four in the morning was when those doors opened and in walked my man. When I heard the doorknob to my bedroom door rattle, I just laid on my side, looking off into space, ignoring him.

"I know you didn't lock this door on me, Celeste," Kadarius huffed, knocking, and trying to open it. I just stayed there silent.

"You know, I got a key."

As soon as I heard the locks kick, he opened the door and walked in. The smell of heavy Versace cologne hit me like a truck. My mind automatically drifted to him trying to drown out the scent of another female. I heard him shuffling behind me, stripping out of his clothes before lying in bed next to me.

"Get out," I huffed, turning around to face him.

"What?"

"Get the hell out of this bed."

"I don't have time to argue with you tonight, Celly."

"Celly my mother fucking ass, Kadarius! Get out of my bed!" I yelled, pulling the covers off of me.

"All because I didn't answer the phone, I was busy."

"Bitc... You know what I'm gonna calm down before I wake my kids. I'm trying not to put my hands on you, Kadarius. Where the hell have you been?"

"After work, I went out for drinks with the guys."

"And didn't tell me shit. I was worried sick about you. Your kids were worried about you. What the hell has gotten into you?"

"Do I trip on your ass when you go out with your friends?

I'd like for you to give me the same decency."

"Fuck that shit. I haven't been out with my friends like that since I had the kids. Don't sit there and fucking lie to me, Kadarius. I know what the fuck I do and don't do. I want you out of my bed tonight because I'm liable to fucking slit your throat while you're sleeping next to me."

"I'm sorry, aight. I should have hit you up and told you I was going out to the bar with the guys."

"It's not even about you going out with your fucking friends, it's about you being my husband Kadarius, and you're failing to realize that. We're drifting apart, and I don't like that feeling. You don't fucking kiss me! You don't fucking hug me, and we haven't had sex in a year! We haven't gone out and done anything together in a year! It's like you're my fucking roommate! When was the last time you looked at me and complimented me?" I yelled, throwing my pillow at him.

I didn't even notice I was hard down in tears venting to him. I tried not to let him see me cry, but I couldn't hold in all these emotions that were spewing out of me like a faucet. He just stood there, staring down at me as if the words I was saying meant nothing to him.

"We both work, Celeste."

"Stop making it about work because it's not fucking work!" I yelled, seeing that he wasn't getting at the points I was throwing at him.

"You know what, get the hell out of this room before I hurt you."

"You really tripping. You know what? I'm gonna go sleep in my man cave and let you get some space to yourself. See you in the morning," Kadarius replied, walking out of the bedroom with a cover and a pillow.

I had to stop myself from yanking the wall lamp off of my nightstand and bashing his ass in the back of his head. He closed the bedroom door, leaving me there in nothing but emotional pain.

Chapter 7: Family First

When she starts bringin' up old dirt
And the fights keep getting worse
Findin' numbers in her purse
Better put that woman first
~Jahiem

I woke up in my man cave pissed. True enough, I was wrong for staying out so late, but Celeste was wrong for putting me out of our bedroom. I had every intention of fucking Reggie for a couple of hours and then coming home, but shit got intense, and I ended up staying out all night. I knew Celeste would be mad, but I didn't think she would be angry enough to kick me out of our bedroom.

My man cave was in the basement. It was where I came to wind down after a long day. I would drink, play video games, and listen to music. It had a fifty-inch flat screen TV, two brown leather sofas, a pool table, and a PlayStation 4. It also had a half bathroom. There were days when I would be down here for hours. Every now and then, I let KJ come down and chill with me.

When I woke up the next morning, I called my secretary to let her know I wouldn't be in today. These sofas I had down here were nice to look at, but horrible to sleep on. I got up to go upstairs to handle my hygiene. I was getting a bathroom built in my man cave, but it wasn't complete yet.

Walking into our bedroom, I noticed Celeste wasn't in the room. Looking at the time, I saw it was about eight o'clock. It didn't matter how late I stayed up, I could never sleep in. With it being this early, I knew Celeste was downstairs with the kids. Once I finished in the bathroom, I went to the kitchen.

"Good morning, everyone," I greeted everybody.

When nobody spoke back, I got worried. Celeste not speaking back was expected, but my kids being silent was a shock.

"KJ and Cassie, did you hear me say good morning?" I asked.

Again, neither one of them said anything. I looked at Celeste to see if she would give me some kind of sign as to what was wrong with them. She turned her head and continued doing what she was doing. Seeing that she wasn't going to help me, I questioned the twins about what was bothering them.

"What's going on guys? You know you can talk to me about anything."

Cassie spoke first.

"Do you not love us?"

"What? Cassie, why would you ask me that? You know I love you. I love you two very much."

"Do you not love mommy?"

"Of course, I do."

"Then why are you never here? Why don't you spend time with us? You were supposed to help me with my science project," KJ spoke.

I felt like shit because I had completely forgotten about his science project. He had been talking about it for weeks now. KJ made me promise I wouldn't forget, and I let him down. That shit hurt my heart.

I knew I was hurting Celeste, but I had no clue my kids were hurting. Not only did I break my promise to my son, I had my daughter questioning if I loved them or not. I had to fix this situation. I apologized for me not being home much and told them I would spend more time with them. Sadly, neither one of them believed me.

To rectify the situation, I called my secretary and told her to give me the rest of the week off. I told Celeste to cancel all her plans for the rest of the week and booked us a flight to Miami. The kids got excited and ran to their rooms to get ready. When they were out of sight, I tried to make things right with my wife.

"Baby, I'm sorry. I promise things will get better between us."

"Kadarius, you haven't been focusing on us, so don't start now. I'm going on this vacation strictly for the kids. If it isn't about them, we have nothing to say to each other," Celeste declared before walking off.

Getting her to forgive me would take a while, so I decided to put it on the back burner for now and focus on the kids. As I was about to go upstairs, my phone rang. When I saw it was Reggie, I sent it to voicemail. Before I could start walking to the stairs, it rang again. I looked to make sure Celeste wasn't around and then answered.

"Hello?"

"What's this I hear about you not going back to work this week?"

"I need to spend time with my wife and kids."

"All that shit we did last night, and you're still worried about your wife and kids?"

"You knew what this was from the beginning. You're just a fling, something to do when I get bored. My wife and kids are my world. I need to stop putting shit before them."

"I'm a fling, huh? That's not what you were saying last night."

Reggie went on and on about why I should leave my wife for him. Since I couldn't raise my voice without somebody hearing me, I hung up on him and turned my phone off. I knew when I turned it back on, I would have to deal with him, but for now, I needed to get my family together.

Chapter 8: Acquainted

Celeste

You got me touchin' on your body
To say that we're in love is dangerous
But girl I'm so glad we're acquainted, oh
I'll get you touchin' on your body
~ The Weeknd

After the stunt Kadarius pulled at breakfast, I couldn't be in the same room with him without wanting to go upside his head with the frying pan. Not once did he ask me what my plans were for the weekend before making plans. It flabbergasted me that he even wanted to play the family man for the weekend. I had a book discussion tomorrow, and I had plans to work on my novel over the weekend since I was preoccupied with planning my event in Seattle, along with taking care of my kids. Even though his intentions may have seemed pure at the moment, here he was thinking about himself and not checking with me.

I shot Raymon a quick e-mail, asking if I could reschedule for his book discussion today because one thing that I didn't take kindly was making plans for them not to go through. As if it felt like I just sent the e-mail seconds ago, Raymon replied to my e-mail with a swiftness. Picking my phone up, I opened his e-mail, and he stated that it was perfectly fine to meet today, and I gave him the time that I would be available.

Going into my walk-in closet, I pulled out my black bare shoulders, Givenchy dress with a pair of Givenchy Chain M-Pumps. Grabbing a washcloth and a towel, I made my way to my bathroom and stripped out of my clothes. Sliding my glass shower door open, I waited for the water to get accustomed to my liking.

"Alexa, play "Love Killa" by B. Smyth."

Music began to play from my Alexa home speaker system. Once the water warmed up to my liking, I got inside and hummed the lyrics of the song. Lathering my Philosophy cinnamon-scented body wash onto my washcloth, I knelt down and started washing my legs.

"Tell me why you always got to lie to a nigga? All I wanted was your honesty 'stead you kept it real with everybody minus me. Trying me!" I sang loudly, feeling that shit.

I stopped singing when the shower glass opened, and Kadarius stepped foot inside, staring down at me. I had the right mind to slam his big-bodied ass into the glass and give him a concussion, but I knew how that would go.

"This house has four bathrooms," I said, rolling my eyes and turning my back to him.

"I wanted to wash up with my wife."

"Yeah, whatever."

"I'm sorry," he apologized, pulling me into him.

Kadarius began planting kisses on my neck, and I couldn't help but let a moan escape my lips. It felt like forever since I felt his touch, and my body was reacting before my mind. As bad as I didn't want him touching me, my body was yearning for him. He reached around me and gripped one of my breasts, brushing his thumb over my erect nipple.

"Do you forgive me?" he asked, pressing his dick against my ass, and sucking on my neck.

I could do nothing but stay quiet because sex wasn't going to make me forgive him. Kadarius changing his ways was what was going to make me forgive him, and I didn't want to give him the wrong idea. I sighed before pushing his hands away and turning to face him.

"What are you doing?" I asked, confused on his intentions. I didn't want him to slowly go back to his old ways just to drift back and go back to what he was doing.

"I'm tryna please my wife."

"What's gotten into you?"

"I'm tryna get into you." He smirked, pulling me into his chest.

"Kadarius, seriously. Why this sudden change?"

"Instead of asking why, enjoy it."

"I'm not enjoying something that's gonna be temporary." I sighed.

"Oh, my fucking god, man! I'm about to get mad tight right now," he groaned, tossing his head back.

"Just answer the question."

"All I'm trying to do is make shit right for you, us, the kids. You know I never miss work. I just feel as if I've been neglecting you and the kids, and I wanna make it up to you, especially you, baby. I've been a real ass, and when you put me out of the bedroom last night, I knew I fucked up. I don't ever wanna make you cry because I vowed never to do that. I love you," Kadarius replied, grabbing my face, and kissing me. I pulled away, not helping myself but to smile.

"Promise me that this is a permanent change and not temporary."

"I promise." He smiled.

"Good."

"Now come give daddy what's rightfully his." He smirked, picking me up and putting my back against the shower. As bad as I've wanted this, I didn't wanna be late for this book discussion.

"Babe, maybe tonight. I have a book discussion to go to in

the next thirty minutes."

"Damn, you don't have time for a quick one."

"Sadly, no, I got you tonight, I promise." I smiled, pecking his lips. Kadarius sighed before letting me down.

Once taking care of my needs, I got out of the shower and dried off before getting dressed. After making sure I moisturized my body in essential rose oil, I curled my straight bundles and let it flow down my back like a river. After kissing and hugging the twins goodbye, I grabbed the keys to my Rolls Royce and got in, driving to the address Raymon gave me.

∞∞∞

I soon found myself in Lenox Hills, and Raymon was standing outside posted up against the stairs. When he saw me getting out of the car, a smile spread across his face as bright as the sun. Closing my door, I got out and walked toward him, extending my hand.

"Hi, it's nice seeing you again, Raymon."

"Likewise, Mrs. Norwood. You look as beautiful as ever." He smiled.

"Thanks so much, and I already told you, you can call me Celeste."

"My bad, I wanna thank you for coming here again, Celeste."

"It's nothing. I can't remember the last time I discussed my book with readers."

"Well, everyone is gonna be excited to see you."

"I can't wait to see them either."

I followed him into his apartment, and when he opened the door, there were up to fifteen people in the living room.

Thankfully, his apartment was spacious, and his decor was beyond exquisite. When everyone saw me coming into the room, they all exclaimed in excitement as if they were little kids in a chocolate factory. I greeted each one of them before Raymon brought me a seat as everyone surrounded me with eager looks on their face. I forgot how exciting and rejuvenating it was to be surrounded by nothing but my supporters.

∞ ∞ ∞

After answering a few questions, discussing my books, signing books, and talking about my upcoming events for three hours, everyone went their separate ways leaving Raymon and I alone in his apartment.

"Well, that was amazing. You guys really enjoy my work, don't you?"

"You have no idea." Raymon smiled, passing me a bottle of water.

"Thanks so much for having me."

"Thanks so much for being here."

"I have a question for you, though?"

"Anything, what's good?"

"Why didn't you ask me any questions about my books?"

"I wanted the members to get to know you and ask their questions first."

"Okay, well now that they are gone, you can ask me anything." I smiled, unscrewing the top off the water bottle, and taking a sip. I leaned on the counter, and he crossed his arms with a smirk, staring at me.

"How do you come up with all this spicy content?"

"Dreams and alone time with my thoughts."

"So, you have dreams about what you write?"

"Sometimes."

"So, when Olivia from *Fire, Ice, and Chains* was being pinned up against the shower, enjoying a threesome with her husband and his twin brother, you dreamed about that?" Raymon asked, walking over to me.

"I'm an incredibly open person with my thoughts, so don't judge me. As a teenager, I was very freaky, and I always pictured my two favorite celebrity crushes having a threesome with me. I knew for a fact it would never happen, and a threesome sounded so good the way I pictured it in my head. So, I decided to write about what I wanted to try." I laughed, thinking of the scene I wrote in the book.

"What about the part where Olivia is giving her husband head in Dubai in the ocean?"

"I'm one of those females who would try adventurous shit. I'm the type of female that would give my husband head under the table at family functions during prayer." I laughed, hating to admit to how much of a freak I was.

"You're a very depictive detailed female."

"Thanks, what's your favorite part of *Fire, Ice, and Chains*?"

"My favorite part is when Olivia and her husband get into an argument, and she tries to leave him."

"When he damn near knocked her ass out?" I laughed, shaking my head.

"Yeah, when he hit her, and she tried to leave, and they had makeup sex. I liked how you described that," Raymon replied, invading my space, placing both hands on each side of me. I looked up at him, frozen.

"You see, I like that aggressive shit, and I can tell you like that aggressive shit because you write about it. I mean, I know sometimes you put yourself in Olivia's shoes. I know you wanna be chained up to a bed butt ass naked, blindfolded, being choked, and fucked. Being taken on such an orgasmic high that your body breaks out into such a ferocious spasm that you get stuck for a few moments, trying to figure out if you really deserve that much pleasure. I liked how you mentioned her husband sucking the cum out of her pussy and spitting it into her mouth, making her swallow it. That shit turned me on, and it made me think about upgrading my game in the bedroom. You, Mrs. Celeste Norwood, knows exactly how to make a man tick," Raymon replied, lifting my chin.

After everything he said, I felt my juices soaking through my panties, and my nipples were hard. Shit, my throat even got dry. I placed my hand on his chest and pushed him back because he was so close to me that I could smell his Versace cologne and the smell of his Crest mint toothpaste on his breath.

"I-I-I uh, I gotta go. It was nice meeting with you, Raymon," I stuttered, trying to gather my bag and my thoughts.

I knew he was looking at me weird because I was technically walking with my legs clenched together. Raymon Stevens was a man that scared me because of his demeanor, but his look and baritone voice attracted me to him like a magnet. I had to get the hell out of there before I smothered his ass with my pussy because I was damn near celibate. I haven't had sex in God knows when, and he was making it hard for me to refrain.

"It was nice getting acquainted with you, Celeste." He smiled, watching me get in my car.

I pulled off and dialed Jolani's number. She answered on the third ring, and from the sound of the police scanner in the background, I could tell she was at work.

"Wassup, girly?"

"We need to talk."

"Oh lord, what happened?"

"I think I almost cheated on Kadarius."

"Almost? Girl, you either did or didn't."

"I didn't, but it felt like it."

"Well, a feeling isn't verification that you did."

"I know."

"He still working like a slave and ignoring you?" She sighed.

"You already know he is."

"Look, if you're not happy, I already told you to divorce him."

"I can't divorce him just because I'm not happy. We have kids together, you know."

"I know, but still, your happiness matters, too."

"My kids' happiness comes before mine, Jojo."

"Okay, whatever you say, sis. Look, I gotta go. Call me when I get off at eight."

"I will."

"Good, love you."

"Love you too, detective." I laughed while hanging up the phone.

It was as if Jolani was the only one I could talk about my marital issues out with. I just couldn't find myself going into more detail about how I almost smothered a man with my pussy that I didn't know. I ran my fingers through my hair, wondering what the hell I got myself into.

Chapter 9: Dangerous Lust

I tried to kiss you
But you never let me miss you
I thought I told you
I'm not him
Look at what you did, nobody forced your hand
~The Weeknd

"I almost had her," I said to aloud myself as I sniffed my hands, hoping they had a hint of Celeste's scent on them. Being that close to her was like a dream come true. The smell of her Guilty by Gucci perfume had me mesmerized. I smelled it as soon as she walked into the room. I hoped and prayed that the scent stayed in my nose all day.

I put my hands on her sides while we were talking to see how far she would let me go. My big hands fit perfectly on her full hips. Even though I only had them on there for a second, I imagined what it would be like to hold them while I had her face down ass up, pounding her from the back. The thought of her soft ass smacking across my pelvis had my dick hard as fuck.

During the discussion, I couldn't pay attention to what was going on because I was too busy focusing on Celeste. The way her words flowed out of her mouth let you know she was a natural at this. When she read scenes from her book, I had to take my mind somewhere to keep my dick from bursting out my pants. That's why I was unable to ask questions. As she was describing the different BDSM scenes her characters partici-pated in, it had me imaging it was us. Having her tied to a table while I smacked her plump ass would be a dream come true.

I've been on edge since she left. I tried to watch porn to calm myself, but it didn't work. I needed some real pussy. Since I couldn't have Celeste, I had to use an alternative. I called up this chick Natalie, who I met at the grocery store that I smashed from time to time. Though she didn't hold a candle to Celeste, she was beautiful. Her five-foot-three frame carried her wide hips and thick thighs well. Up top, she was blessed with a pair of succulent double D breasts. When I first saw her, I thought they were fake. I found out they were real when we were at The Westin downtown getting it in.

We usually had our sexual rendezvous at a hotel, but this time I told her to come to one of my cribs. I had an apartment for business reasons and my home for personal reasons, which was ducked off a little far from the city. I was an adventurous man, so I couldn't live my life here in New York with only one spot. The things I wanted to do to her could only be done in my basement I nicknamed "The Dungeon". There I had every kind of sexual item you could think of—whips, chains, gags, butt plugs, blindfolds, along with several vibrators. I made sure everything was cleaned and ready for her arrival.

∞ ∞ ∞

An hour later, Natalie was at my house, and we were in the dungeon getting ready for the festivities.

"Damn, you a freak!" Natalie exclaimed when she saw everything.

"Maybe just a little bit," I replied.

I strapped her to the table on her stomach after removing her clothes and explaining the rules. Though I hoped she didn't hear it, I told Natalie her safe word was fire. Everything went smoothly at first. I used the vibrators to get her pussy wet, and the butt plugs to open her asshole some. We had never done anal, but tonight every hole she had was fair game.

Everything was going fine until I got out the paddle.

"Umm, what are you about to do with that?" she asked me.

"You've been a bad girl, and you need a spanking," I replied.

"Nah, I'm good."

Not listening to what she said, I reared back and smacked her as hard as I could.

"Fire!" Natalie yelled as loud as she could.

Ignoring what she said, I smacked her a couple more times. She again yelled fire and continued to. Her yelling was killing my vibe, so I got the gag ball and put it in her mouth. Once it was secure and it muffled her cries, I continued. After ripping her panties off, I plunged my dick inside her pussy.

"Oh, Celeste, this pussy is so wet," I moaned.

Natalie turned and looked at me. I'm quite sure she wondered why I called her another woman's name. I told her we were role-playing and kept digging in her guts. I closed my eyes and pictured Celeste moaning my name.

"Deeper, Raymon! I wanna feel you deep in this pussy. Fuck me, Raymon," Celeste told me.

"Damn, Celeste. I knew this pussy was gonna be good."

"Choke me, baby! Choke me hard."

I put my hands around Natalie's throat. The more I dug in her pussy, the harder I choked her. I kept doing this until I filled her with my cum.

"Damn, that was good," I told Natalie.

After pulling out of her, I took the gag out of her mouth. When I did, I noticed she was just lying there. Her body was still, and it didn't look like she was breathing.

"Natalie? Natalie, baby, what's wrong?" I said as I shook her.

When I didn't get a response, I panicked. I must have choked her too hard. *Fuck!* I started pacing back and forth. My first thought was to call 911, but I decided against it. That meant me going to jail and going to jail meant losing Celeste. I paced around the room until I decided to get rid of her body.

There was a garden in my backyard that I started a few months ago in remembrance of my mother. When it got dark, I went out there and dug a deep hole. Once I was content with it, I went back inside to get the body. I wrapped Natalie up in some black trash bags, drugged her outside, and threw her in it. I took the dirt and buried her.

Once I got back inside, I bleached the entire room. While I doing that, I was thinking about what I had done. Killing Natalie was never my intention. I just got caught up in the moment. It would never happen again, though.

After I was satisfied with my clean-up job, I went upstairs and e-mailed Celeste. I thanked her for doing the discussion and asked if I could send her some lunch the next day. It was late, so I didn't expect her to respond. I don't care what I had to do. Celeste Norwood would be mine.

Chapter 10: Heart Full of Rage

Kadarius

She's starin' at me,
I'm sittin', wonderin' what she's thinkin'.
Nobody's talkin',
'Cause talkin' just turned into screamin'.
And now is I'm yellin' over her,
She's yellin' over me.
All that that means
Is neither of us is listening,
~Ne-Yo

I walked over to Celeste, as she stared out at the ocean view in the expensive hotel where we were staying. I wrapped my arms around her waist and kissed her cheek. Just seeing how happy and worry-free her and the kids were, brought joy to me. Today was our last day in Miami, and I wanted to make it memorable for them. I planned on taking them shopping, out to eat, and on a boat ride before we headed back home.

"Morning beautiful." I smiled, pulling her close, inhaling the scent of her shea butter moisturizer. She decided on giving the fake hair a break on our mini-vacation, and every time I looked at her in her natural state, I realized what made me so sprung when it came to her.

"Morning, babe." She smiled, placing her hands on top of mine.

"How long have you been up? You look like you've already been out."

"I decided to take a stroll on the beach. I've been up for a minute now."

"Damn, without me?"

"I wanted to go alone for a reason." She laughed.

"Alright, I understand that."

"What time are we heading home? I know for sure the kids are enjoying themselves, so breakfast at that restaurant we passed by every day sounds good."

"I got something planned for us already."

"Oh really?" she replied, turning around to face me.

"Yes, really, I wanted to make our last day here memorable."

"That's good, considering that you don't think I've been watching you."

"How you mean?"

"I mean, I've seen you step away to take calls the entire time we were here, and I just stood by like it didn't bother me when it did. The only reason I didn't show my ass is because the kids are enjoying themselves, and I didn't wanna ruin that for them. You promised me you wouldn't take any calls, Kadarius." Celeste sighed, shaking her head.

I just stood there, looking down at her, not knowing how to explain myself. She was right, and I hate that she was right. Reggie would call me nonstop, and it was eating me up inside to ignore him. I would always act as if I had to do something so I would be able to get on the phone with him, and it wasn't my intention. Reggie knew how vital this vacation was for my family and me, and yet, he still blew me up. I asked him not to contact me until I returned home, and he disobeyed that.

Part of me wanted to cut him off, but what we had together was such a burning connection that you could feel the heat from miles away. I knew that Celeste would confront me about this, and that was the last thing I needed. I just didn't know that she caught onto what I was doing. It was like an unbeatable game with Reggie and Celeste. They both wanted my attention fully, and I just couldn't do that without neglecting the other. I loved my wife with everything in me, but Reggie had this hold on me that I couldn't leave from.

"It was an important call. You know I told you this vacation was about us." I said, letting her go.

"If it was so much about us, then why is it so hard for you to put that damn phone down. Not once, have I laid my hands on my phone since we landed in Miami, and watching you is like watching a crackhead be locked in a glass box unable to get his daily fix."

"Did you just call me a crackhead."

"If the mother fucking shoe fits, then yes, Kadarius, you're a fucking crackhead. There ain't that much work in the got damn world. Who have you been on the phone with?"

"It was business. I don't even know why we're having this conversation again."

"Just business, huh? If it was business, then why were you on the phone for damn near two hours. I heard your phone ring last night, and I felt you get out of the bed. I know you left the room to get on that goddamn phone. My mama didn't raise no damn dummy."

"Look, can we not do this." I sighed, walking over to the bed, and sitting down.

"That's what the hell I ask you not to do. I asked you not to do this, while we were out here trying to fix us. Who the fuck was on the phone with you?"

"Nobody important."

"Must have fucking been somebody because when we were about to have sex, you stopped and made up a fucking lie to go take your call in the bathroom. When you came out of the bathroom, you didn't even wanna touch me after you got off that phone. So, you got some explaining to do."

"I can never get a fucking break with you."

"Surprise motherfucker, ain't no breaks when you married me, and you know that, so answer me."

"You act like I'm the only motherfucker in this marriage who's addicted to working. What about your ass, huh?"

"What about me? Because I've been by your side since day fucking one, and I have never gotten the same support you barely gave me!" Celeste yelled, walking over to me. I had to grab her hands because I knew she was tempted to hit me. Her fist was balled up, and she was huffing like a bull who was stuck in a red room.

"There have been plenty of fucking nights that I left work early to spend time with you! There have been plenty of fucking nights to where I had to order fucking takeout for the kids and me! All because you were stuck in your got damn room writing books! I supported your shitty ass career since day one, and now that I'm off the ground and running, you don't wanna support me! I stood by your fucking side when you were selling those dusty ass copies of your book out of the back of your beat-up ass 2001 Honda Accord! So, don't for one got damn second say that I barely supported you when I did!"

"My shitty ass career, huh?" She laughed to herself, yanking her arm out of my grasp.

"You heard me."

"Well, my shitty ass career got you your first fucking whip, My shitty ass career paid off all of our fucking loans when we were in debt, and my mother fucking shitty ass career is the got damn reason you are where the fuck you are now! Unlike you motherfucker, I had to work hard to get to where I am today! I worked my ass off like a dog to make sure our family was straight! You were the bitch in this relationship because I fucking took care of us! Your ass was so focused on becoming a football player that you didn't even pay attention to the relationship you had with me. I supported that bullshit ass career you tried to get off the ground, and I was the one who helped you get that fucking firm! You must have forgotten all those loans I paid off for your ass after graduation. So, don't ever in your life, disrespect me like that again."

"Fuck you!" I spat, trying to get up and walk off.

The next thing I knew, Celeste drew her fist back and struck me so hard that I stumbled back into the wall. She was about to run up on me and try to fight me until the kids came out from the adjoined room interrupting us.

"Why are y'all yelling so loud?" KJ asked, letting out a yawn.

Cassie just stood there, probably with the same question on her mind. Her eyes were barely open, and she looked aggravated with everyone in the room. I looked over to Celeste, and she shook her head, grabbing her purse.

"Y'all go put on your shoes."

Once Cassie realized the serious tone in her mother's voice, she wasted no time, throwing on a pair of slides and coming back out. Celeste grabbed both of their hands and walked out, leaving me in the hotel.

I messaged my jaw, which was getting even more swollen by the minute. Celeste's ass must have had the power of God in her hands to make my entire left side of my face numb with one hit. I knew I was gonna trigger her, and I didn't even mean to trigger her. We were going down the wrong path right when I thought we were doing good. I sighed and looked in the mirror, already knowing that I would get side eyes for my swollen face when I walked out. I grabbed my wallet and made my way downstairs to the bar that the hotel had. Finding a seat. I sighed and messaged my jaw.

"What can I get for you?" the bartender asked.

"A Mai Tai."

"Coming right up."

Once she fixed my drink and slid it to me, I felt a hand on my shoulder. Turning around, I raised my eyebrows in confusion, seeing Reggie stare at me.

"The fuck are you doing here?" I asked, clenching the glass so tight that it almost shattered.

"I'm here for you."

"If my wife sees you, it's gonna be my ass and yours."

"Your wife left."

"What?"

"While I was pulling in, she was pulling out, and she looked mad as hell."

I got up from my seat and ran off to the front with Reggie on my trail. When I noticed our car wasn't in our paid parking spot, my blood grew to a boiling point. I didn't know if I was more upset with Celeste for possibly leaving me because I knew nine times out of ten that her ass was headed back to New York, or if I was more pissed at Reggie for popping up unannounced like he was doing.

Chapter 11: What He Won't Do, Another Will

Two Days Later

I tried, but I can't stop thinking 'bout you
And your body, touchin' my body
I fuckin' lose it, girl I don't know what to do
Am I dreamin'? What am I seein'?
I can't believe it. It's just too good to be true
~SIR

It's been two days since I left Miami with the kids. During these two days, Kadarius hasn't come home, and I didn't give a fuck if he did or not. He still had me livid. I wanted to beat the shit out of him, but the kids saved his ass. I was more shocked that he said what he said, then him yelling at me. All I wanted was for him to tell me the truth, and he made the argument into something different. After what he told me, divorce was sticking to my mind like duct tape. I loved this man, but it was sad to say that I wasn't in love with him anymore and it hurt. I thought our mini vacation was supposed to be a start to fixing our issues, but it wasn't.

"You okay?" Charlotte asked.

After telling my sister and my best friends what went down in Miami, they decided to get me out of the house while the kids were in school. My sister wanted to beat his ass as badly as I did. Charlotte, Laurel, and Jolani decided that they wanted to do brunch to talk more about what happened, and I knew I needed to get it off my chest.

"Yeah, I'm fine," I replied, taking a sip of my Sauvignon

from my wine glass.

"Don't look like it," Jolani commented.

"Well. I am, I promise. I'm just thinking."

"Thinking about what?" Laurel, my other best friend, asked.

"Just stuff, I don't feel like talking about it."

"Okay, I respect that but don't shut us out like you used to. You know how you get when you shut everybody out," Charlotte said.

"I know." I sighed.

"Okay, if you know, then spill it, bitch."

"I think Kadarius is cheating on me," I revealed, downing the rest of the wine from my glass, and leaning back in my seat.

"Okay, then cheat back, the fuck!" Charlotte retorted.

"That's little kid shit, I'm not cheating back, especially since I'm not sure."

"You wanna walk in on him fucking another bitch? The fuck you mean since you're not sure? That gut feeling ain't no joke, and you better follow it. Now go out and dress nice and cop you a new nigga."

"I'm not doing that, Charlotte."

"See, you get that loyal shit from mama and daddy. Uncle Louise taught me the game. I'm not gonna sit there and let no motherfucker do me dirty."

"I'm gonna file for divorce. I'm gonna tell him if he won't tell me what the fuck is going on with him, then I'm gonna divorce him."

"That's a good idea, too," Laurel chimed in, rolling her eyes just hearing Kadarius' being talked about.

"I guess, but hey, I'm about to go use that bathroom. I'll be back."

They nodded okay before I stood up and made my way inside the cafe. I really didn't even have to use the bathroom, I just wanted time to think about what I was gonna do about Kadarius, and the advice they were giving me wasn't helping at all.

While walking to the ladies' room, I spotted Raymon sitting at a table in the corner, sipping from his cup and reading a hardcopy of my book. I thought people forgot about my old work, but here he was reading one of my old novels. I walked over toward him and cleared my throat, getting his attention. He looked up and smiled at me, licking his plump lips. This man's sex appeal was on ten thousand, and it should be a crime to be as fine as he was.

"How are you doing, Celeste?" he asked, staring into my eyes.

"I'm fine. I thought I would just stop by and speak. How are you?"

"I'm doing amazing."

"Oh, amazing, huh? Somebody must have come up on some good news."

"Nah, just seeing you made my day even better," he replied, placing his hand on top of mine.

"Oh wow, well, I'm glad I made your day better. I see you reading my first book."

"I am, and I'm impressed. You are one hell of an author Mrs. Norwood, and I'm intrigued by you."

"Intrigued by me?" I asked, breaking out into a huge smile.

"Yeah, I am. I'm not even about to sit here and act like there's not a graceful alluring woman standing in front of me. I know your married and all, but since I met you, I've wanted to get something off my mind. I'm far from a disrespectful man, so do I have permission to tell you?"

I couldn't help but stand there and smile like a little girl standing in front of her crush. It was as if the compliments and the way Raymon was staring at me, dragged me in. Even after being at his home, him describing scenes in my book drew me crazy.

"Speak your mind," I encouraged, coming closer to him.

"Every time I look at you, I just wanna do things to you. I wanna hold you and touch you, and I wanna do things to you that I doubt your husband does to you. You're a beautiful woman with a good head on your shoulders, and I love that. Brains and beauty are hard to come around, and even though you married, I could do things that he won't do to you. I'm very observant when it comes to reading a woman's mind and body. When you were at my place, and I was up on you, you didn't immediately push me away, so I know that your boy back home isn't pleasing that body of yours. This is just something that I needed to get off my chest. I hope what I said doesn't change the way you view me."

I was so stunned by how Raymon read me that I couldn't find anything bad to say to him. I was far from a judgmental person, but this was new to me. I never had a man read me the way he did, and just from how slow and smooth his baritone voice sounded, my girl downstairs was going into hyper drive. I felt that throbbing sensation between my legs, making me bite my lip. I took the book from his hands and closed it before leaning in and whispering in his ear.

"You talk a big game, show me how much better you are than my husband," I replied, gripping his thigh, and walking off to the bathroom.

It was as if the bathroom door didn't even have time to close before Raymon came in after me. He locked the door and walked over to me, looking down at me, licking his lips.

"I'm not a man who likes to be teased. Tell me you want it," Raymon demanded, grabbing me by my waist and pulling me into his chest.

"I want it."

As if those were the magic words, Raymon lifted me and placed me on top of the countertop, pulled my dress up, and opened my legs. I bit my lip as his enormous hands messaged at my inner thighs. When I felt his thumb brush against my already drenched pussy, my body shuddered from his touch. He pulled my blue lace panties off, before kneeling and looking up at me, causing my heart to beat a thousand miles per minute. When I felt him lift me on his shoulders with ease, he latched onto my second set of lips, making me gasp. I grabbed his head and pushed it further, as he sucked and kissed on my clit, making me moan. My breathing hitched as he feasted on my pearl as if it were his last supper, and he was on death row.

"Oh, fuck! Right there!" I groaned, tightening my legs around his head. He leaned me up against the wall and placed two of his fingers inside me while his tongue was still attached to my clit. The faster he pumped in and out of me, I felt myself coming to my peak.

"I'm about to cum!" I warned him, trying to get him to put me down, but he buried his face deeper into me.

As soon as his tongue plunged into my G-spot, I came so hard I thought I almost drowned him. My eye began to twitch from the pleasure before they sooner rolled to the back of my head. My legs were now shaking, dangling over his shoulders. He was still fingering me, this time slowly.

"Celeste, you good in there?" Charlotte questioned, knocking on the bathroom door.

I was so stuck on my orgasmic high that I couldn't even find the words in me to speak. I couldn't even figure out what Raymon said, because as soon as words left his mouth, it caused vibrations on my clit.

"Yes!" I yelled in ecstasy.

"Damn, okay, we thought your ass fell in the toilet or something. We about to leave, so come on."

Raymon licked me clean before placing me on my feet. As soon as my feet touched the ground, I thought I was gonna fall. I looked up at him, seeing that my juices coated his beard like water. I stood back before suddenly feeling the regret wash over me. Did I really just let this man eat me out in the bathroom of a cafe? Did I just cheat on Kadarius? I pulled my skirt down and tried to walk off, but he grabbed me.

"You good?" he asked.

"No, I'm not good. This was all a mistake. We shouldn't have done any of that. Look, I'm sorry for leading you on and pushing you to do this. I gotta go," I replied, trying to walk off again but Raymon grabbed me, and this time he grabbed me by my throat and kissed my sloppily, making sure he made me taste myself.

He bit my lip and pulled away, making me want more, but I couldn't get anymore. I pushed him away, walked out of the bathroom, meeting Charlotte and Laurel outside, doing the walk of shame.

Chapter 12: Fulfilling Fantasies

Raymon

I tasted her! I actually tasted her! These words played over and over in my head as I headed home from the cafe. I had been to that cafe on several occasions to have my usual mocha latte and onion bagel while reading a book, but none of my trips had ever been this eventful. Since Celeste had been on my mind, I decided to read one of the first books she had ever published. Well, reread it because I had read it before. It wasn't on the same level as *Fire, Ice, and Chains*, but it was still a good read.

I was so into the book that I didn't even notice Celeste walk over to me. Though she had stress written all over her face, she was still gorgeous. While we were talking, I felt a rush of heat. I knew it was my lust for her, so I decided to "shoot my shot" as they say. When she didn't object, I immediately made my move. Eating pussy wasn't something I was particularly fond of, but for Celeste, I would do anything. Her pussy tasted like a fresh jar of honey. It was so sweet. I never wanted the taste of it to leave my tongue.

I just knew I was finally about to plunge inside the pussy that I had been craving since the first day I laid eyes on her, but her sister knocked on the door and killed that. In my mind, Celeste would have told her to leave without her. Not only did she leave with her, she told me everything we did was a mistake. To most guys, that would have been the end. However, I was a different breed. Her telling me it was a mistake made me want her more.

$$\infty\infty\infty$$

The next day I sat at my desk, trying to come up with a way to get in Celeste's pussy. Trying to convince her flat out was out of the question. I needed to do something big. I glanced down at the book I was supposed to be reading for our next book discussion, and that's when an idea popped in my head. I immediately went to my book club's Gmail account to send an e-mail:

Dear Mrs. Norwood,

It was a pleasure meeting you at our last book discussion. We enjoyed your discussion so much that we have decided to go ahead and discuss part two of your book. Are you available this Saturday at around six p.m.? I apologize for the short notice. Please respond at your earliest convenience.

Sincerely yours,

Raymon Stevens
Club President

After reading what I wrote to make sure it sounded professional before pressing send, I hoped and prayed since it was about business, she would respond. I checked a few more things online before getting ready to get off the computer. Before I did, I got an alert, letting me know I had a new e-mail. When I opened it, I saw it was Celeste confirming that she would be at the book discussion.

"Yes!" I yelled out as I went to my Marriott Bonvoy app to book a suite at the Marriott Marquis for Saturday night. Once it was booked, I placed an order for two dozen long stem red roses to be picked up Saturday afternoon.

Once it was confirmed that they would be ready, I left to go to Victoria Secret to get some lingerie for Celeste. I had no clue what her size was, but I still wanted to get something. If nothing else, she would appreciate the fact that I got it. I also wanted to pick up some body spray for her. Hopefully, this would show her how special she was to me.

Saturday Evening

I was on pins and needles waiting for Celeste to arrive. Thursday evening, she sent me an e-mail asking where the discussion would be held. When I told her the hotel name and the address, she immediately wanted to know why it was being held at a hotel. I made up a lie about the host having a flood at their home, and none of the other members could fill in since it was last minute. I hadn't heard from her since then, so I wasn't sure if she would show.

I told her to be here at 6 o'clock, and it was now 5:30. Our food had been brought up from the kitchen a little while ago. Not knowing what she would like to eat, I ordered a variety of sandwiches and some salads along with some bottled water. Asking for water sounded odd when I was trying to get some pussy, but I was big on staying hydrated, and we were about to work up a sweat. We had a suite that consisted of a living room, kitchen, and a king-size bedroom. I planned to make love to her all over this room. I had been working to make sure everything I needed was perfect and in place since I checked in.

At about 5:45, there was a knock at the door. Since I had ordered nothing else, I knew it was Celeste. I checked my appearance in the mirror and then went to the door.

"Hello, Celeste! Come in. How are you?"

"I'm fine. Umm…where is everyone?"

"It's just us," I declared.

"Just us? You said this was a book discussion."

"It is a book discussion. I want you to sit on that bed and read to me while I suck on that sweet pussy of yours," I said while licking my lips.

"Raymon, we can't do this. I have to go," she replied while rushing to the door.

I knew this would be her initial reaction. I wasn't ready to give up just yet.

"Celeste, wait! Listen, I understand you don't want to do this because of your husband, but you need to do something for yourself. I could tell by the way you reacted to my touch the other day that your body hasn't been getting any attention. That pussy exploded in my mouth like it had been holding that shit in forever. I'm not trying to be your secret boyfriend or anything like that. I just want to be the one who makes your body feel good. Can I do that? Can I make you feel good?"

She took her hand off the doorknob and turned to face me. Her face held a blank state, but I could tell she was thinking about what I said. Rather than wait for her to make up her mind, I took her hand and led her over to the sofa. I took the bag I assumed contained the swag she had for the members of the book club and sat them on the coffee table. I made a mental note to pay her for the items later.

I sat her down, kneeled in front of her, and placed a few kisses on her lips. When she didn't stop me, I started passionately kissing her. Her lips were soft as pillows, and I never wanted to take my mouth off them. Next, I slowly started removing her clothes. Once she was naked, I handed her a book.

"You going to read to daddy while he sucks on this pussy?"

"We both know that the last thing I will be focused on is a

book, so put it down. You said you wanted me, so take me. I have to pick my kids up in a few hours."

Not wanting to waste any time, I opened her legs and feasted on her pussy. It tasted just as good if not better than it did the last time. Since we didn't have much time, I decided to cut my tasting short. I picked her up and took her in the bedroom where I had rose petals across the bed. There were candles, but I was so nervous that I forgot to light them.

"This is beautiful. You did all this for me?"

"Yes, baby. I wanted our first time to be special."

Instead of responding to me, Celeste pulled my pants down and took me in her mouth.

"Fuck!" I moaned out.

My dick felt so good in her mouth. She was sucking my dick like a pro. It got so good that I had to sit down on the bed because my knees were getting weak. As bad as I didn't want her to stop, I had to stop her so that I wouldn't cum quickly. I pushed her off me and laid her on the bed before grabbing a condom off the dresser.

Once the condom was on, I climbed in the bed where Celeste's open legs were waiting. I slid two fingers in her pussy while kissing her to tease her a little.

"Stop playing with me, Raymon!"

"Feisty, aren't we?" I asked before sliding my dick inside her.

I had no idea what heaven felt like, but I'm quite sure being inside her pussy was close to it. For the next two hours, we fucked on every inch of that room in several different positions. I knew sex with her would be good, but I never imagined it would be this good. When it was time for her to leave, we said our goodbyes, and I made her promise this wouldn't be the last time. She told me she couldn't make any promises, but she would try.

When she left, I took a shower. Since I booked the room for the night, I would stay here. While I was in the shower, I felt myself having flashbacks of the fuck session Celeste and I had. I had planned to take things slow and make sweet love to her, but all that changed when I slid inside her. I couldn't wait until I was in it again. I know Celeste was married and all, but one way or another, she would be mine.

Chapter 13: The Grass Ain't Greener

Kadarius

Two Weeks Later

You used to be the one to talk to on the side
Waiting for my love to break up
It's crazy how your ass can walk through every night
Acting like you been a player
That grass ain't greener on the other side
~Chris Brown

What was supposed to be a wonderful trip ended up being horrible. Not only did Celeste storm off with my kids, but Reggie showed his ass up. I was livid when I saw him. I wasn't answering his calls because I was trying to fix my marriage and bond with my kids. His constant calling and texting ruined that for me. I tried my best to play it off so that Celeste wouldn't get suspicious, but that shit didn't work. I should have known it wouldn't. Not only was Celeste a smart woman, but she had also written stories about men cheating and ways they get caught. Therefore, in a sense, I was acting out a story.

Reggie thought my wife leaving meant we would stay in Miami on some romantic shit. Wrong! I hopped my ass on the first flight back to New York. I knew there was no way Celeste would let me back to the house, so I checked into a hotel. A couple of days later, Reggie found me and begged me to come stay at our condo. I wasn't sure how the hell he found me. There are tons of hotels in the city of New York and the surrounding boroughs, so I could have been anywhere. Come to think about it. I wasn't sure how he found me in Miami, either. I don't have my location on my phone, so he couldn't have done it that way.

When I refused to go with him, he took it upon himself to move in the hotel with me. That lasted about three days before I agreed to go to the condo. Not that I wanted it, but at least there I could go to another room as opposed to being cramped up in that hotel room. The first few days were fine. We made love before work in the morning, watched movies, and he cooked us dinner every night. Reggie was a good cook but nothing like Celeste.

During dinner last night, I was distant. I had to figure out a way to get back to my kids. They were my world and being away from them was killing me. Before this happened, I thought I enjoyed being with Reggie more than I did my wife. I thought the kids were the only reason I was still with her. Being away from her made me realize I was wrong. True enough, Reggie was fun to be around, and the sex was bananas. However, as the saying goes, there is nothing like a woman's touch. Rolling over into the soft arms of the woman who thinks the world of you is the best feeling in the world. That's not to say that Reggie didn't care about me. He just didn't care about me the way my wife did.

"Kadarius, have you heard anything I said?" Reggie asked me while we were lying in bed together.

"How did you know where I was?" I asked, not caring about what he had just said.

"What do you mean?"

"In Miami, how did you know where to find me? How did you know what hotel I was at?"

"You told me when you first got there. See…"

He took out his phone and showed me a picture I had sent him of me in front of the hotel. Under it, there was a message telling him how we would have to make a trip there together. I had completely forgotten about that. That still didn't explain how he found me here.

"How did you find me here?"

Chapter 14: I Wanna Be Your Man

How you feel about me, can't live without me
They don't know, ow that pretty thing
cream when you think about me
They don't know, you've been staying
in my condo 'bout a month
It's a key up on your chain, when you goin'
through some things, escape whenever you want
They don't know, how I hit it by the fire
And your legs stretch wider, and your chest gets tighter
~Trey Songz

"Oh my god, I can't remember the last time I've been to a club," I spoke, walking through the doors with Laurel and Charlotte behind me.

I looked around to see everybody dancing up on one another while the shining lights flashed on their sweaty glistening skin like diamonds. The smell of alcohol and weed hit my nose like a truck. We made our way to the bar and grabbed three free seats.

"Bitch, you look nice. I know I said this in the car, but damn girl. Belly on flat, ass on fat, twins where? I know you used to dress like a bad bitch before all this marriage issue shit, but girl, you look amazing. Look at you glowing and shit," Charlotte complimented, nudging my shoulder.

I could do nothing but smile and looked down at my outfit. I sported a gold Saint Laurent V-neck halter neck mini dress, a pair of Tom Ford Padlock 105mm sandal heels, and my twenty- eight-inch body wave bundles flowed down my back like a river. I decided on light makeup, so I only did my eyebrows and applied lip gloss, and I sported a custom diamond choker with a matching pair of earrings.

"Thanks, sis, I thought I would step out looking like a meal tonight."

"Well, you did that," the bartender chimed in, walking up and eyeing me up and down.

"Thanks."

"What can I get you, beautiful ladies, to drink?"

"Can I just get a martini?" Charlotte requested.

"I'll get a White Russian," Laurel ordered.

"I'll get a Paloma, heavy on the tequila, please." I smiled.

He nodded and turned around to fix our drinks. Once he prepared our drinks, he turned to us and placed them in front of us.

We rapped the lyrics to "21 Questions" by 50 Cent while sipping on our drinks. I pulled out a fifty-dollar bill to try to pay for our drinks, but I felt a familiar touch on my hand. As I looked up, my eyes grew wide, seeing Raymon looking down at me. He handed the bartender a hundred-dollar bill and licked his lips, looking me up and down. It couldn't have been a coincidence seeing him here, but it felt as if we were bumping into one another often, and I didn't like that, especially after what we did at the Marriott. I didn't have any plans to do what we did ever again. Raymon drew me in like a firefly, and I knew it was wrong, but I had to resist the temptation.

"Well, well, well, Celeste, you're looking as beautiful as ever," he complimented, trying to touch my thigh, but I pushed his hand away. The last thing I needed was Laurel and my sister in my business.

"Thanks, what are you doing here?"

"I needed a change of scenery. I got tired of being at the

cafe."

"Oh." I laughed awkwardly.

"Uh, Celly, who this?" Charlotte quizzed, eyeing Raymon like he was a piece of meat.

"This is Ra—"

"Raymon Stevens, a good friend of hers," he interrupted, extending his hand to shake Charlotte's hand. She and Laurel shook his hand, and they gave me a look that I knew too well.

"Raymon, this is my sister Charlotte, and my best friend Laurel."

"It's nice meeting you beautiful ladies. Celeste, can I talk to you real quick?"

"I don't know, Raymon."

"It'll be quick, I promise."

I sighed and gave my sisters a look indicating that I would be back. Raymon tried to grab my hand to guide me through the crowd, but I didn't want him touching me at all. The last thing I needed was us fucking in the bathroom. Once we got to a quieter area, I crossed my arms and gave him a stern look.

"Make it quick," I said, looking up at him.

"I missed you. Why haven't you been answering my calls and e-mails?"

"Raymon, I told you we're not doing any of that again. I'm marrie—"

"I don't wanna hear about your got damn husband. Apparently, he's not here, and he isn't making you happy. Celeste, I make you happy, and I can tell I do. We both know I make you happy, and we both know your marriage is crumbling apart."

"Look, you're an amazing person, and you're wonderful to be around. I wanna thank you for being there for my career since day one, and I wanna thank you for making me take risks that I never in a million years would have taken. But Raymon, this thing that you and I have going on has to stop, and it stops tonight."

"You don't mean that," he countered, trying to touch me, but I pushed his hand away.

"I do mean it."

"Let me guess. You're getting things back on track with your husband, right? I'm telling you I can make you happy, I can make you feel things you've never felt before. *I know you*, and I know what you need to do. What you need to do is stop playing and do what you've wanted to do since we did what we did in the hotel."

"No, I'm not. I'm tired of men in general thinking they can control me. My father and my husband have all controlled me, and I'll be damn if I sit here and let you control me."

"I'm not trying to control you."

"You trying to tell me what I need to do. I'm a grown ass woman Raymon, and—"

Raymon grabbed my face roughly and attacked my lips. I then felt him lift my dress and try to put his fingers in my under-wear. I pushed him back and slapped the shit out of him, catching him off guard. I straightened out my clothes and wiped my lips.

"Never come near me again."

"Celeste, I'm so—"

"I mean it, Raymon, stay away from me," I demanded, trying to walk away, but he grabbed my arm.

As soon as I was about to say something, Kadarius walked up and pulled me away from Raymon, sizing him up. Raymon had him beat by a couple of inches, but I was shocked that he was there. This was the thing that I didn't want to happen.

"Put your hands on my wife one more time, and I'mma

fuck you up, you hear me," Kadarius warned.

Raymon had this crazy look in his eyes that scared me a bit, and even though Kadarius was built bigger than him, he wasn't backing down. Raymon looked at me once more before walking off. Kadarius turned to me and shook his head.

"What are you doing here? Where are my kids?" he asked.

"I know the fuck you not asking me this right now. Why the fuck are you here? As a matter of fact, I don't even wanna know. I don't want shit to do with you, Kadarius," I replied, trying to walk off, but he grabbed me.

"Stop, wait. Look, I'm sorry."

"Feed that sorry bullshit to the birds, Kadarius."

"Celly—"

"Don't fucking *Celly* me. I'm liable to take my heel off and bash you in your shit. Get out of my face, Kadarius."

"Baby, I'm terribly sorry, and I've been suffering these past two weeks without you. I miss you, and I miss the kids. The time that I haven't been with you, I've had time to realize how much I need you in my life."

"Save that sappy shit for somebody who cares."

"You don't have to believe me Celeste, but I'm asking you to give me another chance. I know I fucked up. and I don't deserve another chance, but I promise I won't ever hurt you again. I never meant what I said back at the hotel."

"Kadarius, leave me alone," I sniffled, feeling genuinely hurt.

As bad as I didn't want to give him another chance, I felt as if I had to because we had kids together. He wiped away my tears and pushed me into the bathroom, locking the door. He pressed his lips against mine, and picked me up, placing me on top of the countertop, spreading my legs.

"I love you," he said, still with his lips pressed against mine.

"I love you too."

"I Wanna Be Your Man" by Zapp and Rogers blasted through the club. It was the same song that Kadarius proposed to me at the skating rink with. He looked at me with those same, daring dark eyes. He slid his pants down and pulled my thong to the side, before pulling me closer and placing his dick at my entrance. Once I felt him ease himself inside of me, I threw my head back and ran my fingers through his fresh waves, biting my lip. He sent slow strokes through my body while sucking and kissing on my neck. He then pulled my dress straps down, exposing my fully erect nipples, I felt a chill go down my spine when he brushed his thumb across it. He then picked me up and placed me up against the wall picking up his pace.

"Fuck! Right there!" I moaned into his ear, clawing at his shoulders.

"You like that, damn you so tight," he groaned, digging his nails into my ass.

I felt myself tightening around him, and by the way his breath hitched, I could tell he was coming to his point as well. We both let out the most orgasmic moans our body could produce and came at the same time. We were so stuck on cloud nine that he still had me pinned up against the wall.

I didn't know what the hell I got myself into, or where my mind would be after leaving this bathroom. Did Kadarius really deserve a second chance? Part of me didn't wanna give him a second chance because fear was in my heart heavy. I was scared that if I gave him another chance, I would be hurt again, and I would look stupid yet again.

Chapter 15: Psychotic Thoughts

Tried to call a million times and no I won't stop (won't stop)
Callin' to apologize, just got my heart stuck (heart stuck)
You found some things you never should have
found, never should have found (but now)
But you found it anyway, you found it anyway
~PARTYNEXTDOOR

I felt myself getting angrier by the moment. I had my ear pressed against the bathroom stall, hearing her moans, wishing it were me. Wishing that I were the one blowing Celeste's back out, having her scream my name. I punched the bathroom door and walked out of the club, fuming.

I headed over to my all black Range Rover and got in, speeding out of the parking lot. I stopped at a nearby gas station and got out, heading inside. Going to one of the coolers, I opened it and pulled out three cans of Budweiser. Grabbing a bag of chips, I went to the register and paid for my items along with twenty in gas. Walking over to the gas tank, I unscrewed the nozzle off of my tank and started pumping my gas.

"You're too sexy to be frowning like that." A woman approached me, wearing lingerie with jean shorts and a fur coat. I assumed she was a hooker by the way she was dressed, along with me not seeing her come from a car.

"Why you worried about me frowning?" I asked, leaning on my car.

"Because I don't like seeing a fine ass man look down. What's your name?"

"Marcus. You?" I replied, giving her a fake name.

"Kylie. Now back to you frowning. I don't like that."

"Then come and make me smile." I smirked. I needed something to get Celeste off my mind, and this right here would have had to do. She smirked back at me and made her way over to the passenger's side of my car.

After I finished pumping my gas, I got in my car and pulled off, making my way to my house. When we pulled up, I killed the engine, and she followed me inside. Closing and locking my front door, I told Kylie to wait on me in my living room while I got myself together. I went to my bedroom and took my Rolex off, along with my gold chain. I unbuttoned my white polo shirt and took it off, showcasing my chest that was painted with tattoos. I changed out of my jeans into some basketball shorts and made my way back into the living room.

I scrunched my face in confusion, seeing that Kylie wasn't there anymore. I walked around my house calling for her and I didn't see her. Heading upstairs, I went toward my room where I did my work. She was walking out of the room, with fear on her face.

"I thought I told you to stay downstairs," I stated, tilting my head. I could feel myself changing mentally. I knew I was about to lash out.

"What the hell did I just see Marcus? Is that C.K Norwood?" she asked, pointing at the room. I had photos of Celeste plastered all over the walls, along with videos of her. I even recorded us, unbeknownst to her, when we were making love at the Marriott.

"Why is that any of your business?"

"I think it's time for me to go."

"Nah, I think you came just in time."

"I'm gonna leave."

"No, you're not."

As soon as she tried to run, I grabbed her by her hair and dragged her down the stairs while she screamed and kicked. I then pulled her into The Dungeon and chained her to the bed.

"You know you hardheaded, right?" I said, stripping her of her clothes.

"You're a fucking lunatic! Let me go! If you touch me, I swear to God I'm calling the cops!" she screamed, tugging at the chains.

"You're the lunatic, I didn't even give you my real name, and you jumped in the car with me." I laughed to myself, going to my drawer, pulling out a condom.

"You're fucking crazy! If you don't let me go—"

"Then what? If I don't, what are you gonna do? I love it when women are aggressive with me."

"I'm gonna call the fucking cops, and you're going to jail! I'm gonna tell them about your little shrine and everything! You're a fucking stalker, and no women will ever willingly want you, especially not her!" she yelled.

Grabbing my red rope from the wall, I walked over to Kylie and wrapped it around her neck, furious. Tying it into a noose around her neck, I ignored her pleads and began strangling her until her face turned red then blue. She tried to gasp for air until there was nothing to grasp for. I didn't even notice I killed her until her eyes bulged out of her head, almost coming out of the socket. I was still so pissed off and mad that I was still pulling the rope until I heard her neck snap.

Walking over to her dead body, I knelt and placed my lips to her ear, "She *does* want me!" I screamed.

I raged, all around my home, throwing things everywhere and screaming in anger. I tore my entire house up, including The Dungeon. I sat in my backyard, drinking the Budweiser I purchased from the gas station.

"She wants me," I said to myself.

I felt my phone vibrate in my pocket. Pulling it out, thinking it was Celeste, I frowned, seeing that it was my wife texting me.

Diana: *I haven't spoken to you in a minute, just checking on you to make sure you're okay. How's therapy going? I know how hard dealing with your condition can be for you, but just know I'm here for you. Whenever you're ready to come home, I'm here.*

I ignored her text and went to Celeste's contact before calling and being sent to voicemail. I threw my phone across the room and yelled, feeling my anger rise by the minute.

Chapter 16: The Big Event

Celeste

Three Months Later

*Then I just sit back and decipher, what they really meant
Cherish these nights, cherish these people
Life is a movie, but there will never be a sequel
And I'm good with that, as long as I'm peaceful
~Nicki Minaj*

The day of my Seattle book event was finally here. My nervousness was at an all-time high. I had done several small book signings at different bookstores, but they in no way could prepare me for this. The Seattle Kickback was an event hosted by a group of authors that lived here. Each year authors from around the world came to sell books and interact with readers. Many of my author friends have been going every year since it started, but this was my first year attending.

From the pictures I had seen, authors took different swag items to give out to readers who purchased books from them. I ordered bookmarks, pens, tumblers, business cards. My table would be decorated with candy, water, and cupcakes. Next to it, there would be a banner with my name and picture that Kadarius ordered for me.

Not only was today the day of the event. I got a call this morning confirming that my book *Fire, Ice, and Chains* would be turned into a movie. I submitted my manuscript to a film company a few months ago and finally heard from them. Things with my career were finally taking off for me. We were set to start casting next month, and I couldn't wait to share the big news with everyone here today. With the way things had been with my husband and me, this distraction was much needed.

Speaking of Kadarius, things between us have been getting a little better. After we had sex at the club that night, he moved back in. Since I wasn't ready to let him back in our bedroom, he slept in his man cave. He started helping more with the kids and did more chores around the house.

What shocked me the most was when he told me he was going to Seattle with me. Attending anything book related was something Kadarius claimed he hated to do. He felt they were boring. You would have thought since his wife is an author, he would attend at least one or two. When he told me that he was coming with me, I thought it was a joke. However, here he is, setting my banner up.

"That looks good," I told him once he was finished.

"I'm glad you like it. I was afraid it wouldn't be big enough. I want it to draw attention to people when they walk in." His gesture was about to bring tears to my eyes. Kadarius had always been a perfectionist, just not when it came to me.

I shook off my urge to cry and began placing my stuff on my table. My original plan was to share a table with another author, but my sister surprised me by buying me a single table.

Looking around the room made me nervous. There were so many well-known authors, and I was just happy being around a crowd of people who were like me, who understood me. When I first started out, I always though I wasn't supposed to be here because I was still building myself. True enough, I had a big reader base. However, my nerves always seemed to go bad at these events because of my anxiety. Even though I had a huge support system and I built my financial stability from the ground up, I still to this day have doubts about myself.

"Shit!" I yelled after knocking all my bottled waters over.

"Celly, baby, calm down. Everything will go well for you. The people will love you!" Kadarius told me before kissing my forehead.

Kissing my forehead always calmed me down for some reason. I thanked him for the words of encouragement and finished setting up my table. After making sure everything was perfect, I took some pictures and sent them to my sister, who was on auntie duty until I returned. When it was time to start, I said a quick prayer and prepared myself.

∞ ∞ ∞

Things started slowly at first, but an hour after it started, the kickback was in full swing. A few of my readers who I communicated with online found me and got signed copies of my book and took pictures with me. I also gained a couple of new readers. Things were going better than I expected.

"Baby, would you go get me something to snack on from the concession stand?" I asked Kadarius.

We would dinner once the event was over, but with the way my stomach was growling, I couldn't wait another three hours. He walked off, and I started placing more water on my table.

"Excuse me, are you C.K. Norwood?" I heard a voice ask me while my back was turned.

"I am," I replied.

"My name is Reggie Kingston. I was asking around for good author recommendations and was sent your way."

"Nice to meet you, Mr. Kingston. I hope that my books will be to your liking."

"It's nice to meet you also. Please, call Reggie. I've never read erotica before. I'm more of a paranormal kind of guy. I'm trying to expand my tastes. *Fire, Ice, and Chains,* huh? Well, if nothing else, the title sure has my attention. How did you come up with it?"

I had been asked that question a million times. I explained to him how it just came to me while I was doing my research on BDSM.

"That's awesome. I'm sure I'll be ready to test some of the scenes out with my boyfriend by the time I'm done reading."

"I've been told that book has that effect on people. How long have you two been together if you don't mind me asking?

"About a year. I love him to death but wish we could spend more time together."

"What is it that prevents you two from spending time together? Work schedules?"

"That and a few obstacles are between us on his end."

"Ah! Gotcha. Well, hopefully, he will remove them so that you two can be together."

"He's hesitant about it, but I've decided that if he doesn't remove them, I will. If I have to do it, it won't be a pretty sight."

There was something about his tone when he said that last part that made me feel uneasy. It sounded threatening. I signed his book, took a selfie with him, and he walked away. My gut told me there was something wrong with that man. However, before I could ponder about what it was, Raymon walked up.

"Nice to see that you're alive and well, considering that you haven't answered my calls or responded to my messages."

"Raymon, I told you what happened between us was a mistake, and it will never happen again."

"And why is that?"

"I have a husband, remember?"

"You weren't worried about your husband when I had your pussy in my face now, were you?"

"You need to leave!"

"But you haven't signed my book yet."

Before I could respond, Kadarius came back with my snacks.

"Sorry, it took so long, sweetheart. The line was long."

"It's okay, baby. I was just about to sign Mr. Stevens' book so that he could go to another table."

"Well, don't let me interrupt."

"You aren't interrupting. Nice to see you again, Mr. Norwood."

"Kadarius. We've met before?"

"Yes. At the club about a couple of months ago. You were so focused on your wife that you might not remember."

"I don't. I apologize."

"It's okay. I was just telling your wife how talented she is and congratulating her on her movie deal."

"Talented she is! I'm not sure who's more excited about this movie, me or her."

The way Raymon said talented let me know he wasn't just talking about my writing. I quickly signed his book and sent him away before he opened his mouth about what happened between us.

I took my snacks from Kadarius and started eating. I felt a pair of eyes on me and assumed it was Raymon. However, when I looked around, I saw that Reggie guy staring a hole in my face. There was something off about him that I couldn't put my finger on, but something told me I would find out what it was soon.

Chapter 17: When Fools Fall In Love

Kadarius

Only you can make all this change in me
For it's true, you are my destiny
When you hold my hand
I understand the magic that you do
~ The Platters

I stood to the side and watched Celeste sign copies of her book, discuss her movie deal, and converse with her supporters. I could do nothing but smile at how happy she was in her surroundings. I never really showed up to these things, but today, I felt as if I had to come. I was trying my best to get things back to how they used to be with Celeste and me.

Even though we weren't officially back in that spot, we were slowly working ourselves back to that place. During our break from one another, I noticed how much I missed my wife and kids. I noticed how it felt to be without them, and that was a feeling I dreaded. I changed my phone number and e-mails because I knew Reggie would try to get in touch with me in any way he could through my old information.

"Hey babe, can you do me a favor and get the other box of books from the trunk of my car?" Celeste asked.

"Yeah, you need anything else?"

"Uh yeah, now that you mention it, please grab my custom stainless-steel cups from the car too, I'm almost out."

"Okay, I got you."

Fishing in my pocket for my keys, I walked out of the

building and made my way to our car. As soon as I got closer, I saw Reggie leaning on the car with an unpleasant look on his face. I had to stop myself from dragging his ass out of the parking lot before I caused a scene.

"The fuck are you doing here?" I quizzed through gritted teeth.

"I'm here to upgrade my library," he answered sarcastically.

"Does it look like I'm trying to be fucking funny with you right now?"

"I personally met your wife. She's one hell of a woman. I can tell you that."

I rushed up to Reggie and jacked him up. My nose flared up, and I felt the vein bulging in my forehead so fast that it felt as if it were about to pop.

"You come near my wife again, and I'm gonna show you better than I can tell you how serious I get for my family. I said we're done, and I meant that."

"You're gonna come back to me, Kadarius. As soon as she fucks up and pushes you away, you'll be right back in my bed."

"I meant what the hell I said. Stay the hell away from my wife, Reggie, and I mean it," I warned letting him go.

"You'll see me again, trust and believe that," Reggie threatened, walking away from me.

I shook my head at him and grabbed what Celeste needed before walking back inside. Walking over to the table, I sat everything down and took a seat.

Once everything started to die down, Celeste and I

gathered our belongings and made our way back to the hotel. After finding out that Reggie was here, the last thing I needed was his ass popping up at the restaurant I planned on taking Celeste to. Celeste and I decided on Hibachi being delivered to our room and decided to watch throwback movies. We were lying in our king size bed, watching *Why Do Fools Fall In Love*.

"Why you so quiet?" Celeste asked, nudging my shoulders.

"No reason, just thinking."

"About what?"

"About you." I smiled, pulling her into my arms.

"What about me?"

"How proud of you I am."

"Thank you. It meant a lot for you to be here with me today."

"I know."

"Mhm, right."

"I'm for real, I'm so proud of you, and I'm happy that I could be your husband. You're a strong independent woman, and I love that about you. For you to be having your book turned into a movie is something that you've been dreaming about for a long time."

"You have no idea how excited I am about that." She smiled, leaning up from my arms and staring me in my eyes.

"I know." I laughed.

"But we are in Seattle for two more days, so what do you wanna do, unless you wanna go back home early?"

"I wanna do whatever you wanna do, baby."

"Mhm, whatever. Right now, I wanna restart this movie."

"Oh my god, please don't Celly."

"You know this is my movie."

"Why?"

"Are you really asking me this?"

"Yes. Why do you like this movie so damn much? I remember when we first started dating, since the rain ruined our date at the park, we decided on a movie night. You sat there and made me watch this movie four times straight in a row. So, what's the deal? You in love with Frankie Lymon or something? Don't get me started on *The* fucking *Five Heartbeats*."

"Uh-uh, don't play me like that." Celeste laughed, playfully punching me in the shoulder.

"I'm for real. What's the deal, though?"

"The chemistry, the love, the deceit, the pain, and the reconciliation. *Why Do Fools Fall In Love* shows how gullible women are with their hearts, yet it shows how weak men are with their hearts. Frankie led all three women on and made them fall in love with him. These women genuinely loved Frankie, but they loved money more, and throughout all of this, Frankie loves the spotlight, and yet he loves them. This movie shows how crazy it is when your heart is being controlled like a puppet. And let's not forget the music, that lil mother fucker can sing. You know how much I love old school classics, and the music in this movie gives me life," she ranted.

"Okay, thank you for the summary of the movie." I laughed.

"Shut up. See, look, this is my part," Celeste replied, getting up and grabbing her phone to use as a mic. The scene where Frankie and Teenagers were singing outside popped up on the screen and Celeste began to dance side to side singing.

"Why do fools fall in love? Why do birds sing so gay? And lovers await the break of day. Why do they fall in love?" she sang, stepping from side to side as if she was a background dancer.

All I could do was sit there and laugh at how jokey she was. The way her natural hair was all over the place like a ferocious lion, the way her smooth face shined without makeup, she looked beautiful, and I couldn't help but stare at her in awe. The fact that she could actually sing drew me in even more into her little charades.

Once she was growing tired, she walked back over to the bed, out of breath from moving so much.

"You're so damn goofy."

"You know I did my thang. You're just jealous that you can't sing." She laughed.

"I know I can't sing." I laughed.

"So, what's the plan for tomorrow?"

"How about we visit the Chihuly Garden and Glass, and then we get something to eat."

"I didn't get a chance to see the Space Needle, so we can do that too. Oh, and I promised the kids I would FaceTime them if we went to the aquarium. You know we gotta take them out when we get back home, right?"

"I know." I laughed, already hearing the twins yelling at me for still not bringing them here with us.

"Look, I'm about to go to sleep, though. I'm tired."

"I knew you were getting tired. It's four in the morning. I don't even know why you even decided to stay up this late."

"I couldn't sleep then, but now I'm tired."

"Of course, you are." I laughed, watching her climb in under the covers.

"So, am I sleeping on the couch tonight, or do I have permission to sleep with you."

She sighed before giving me a hesitant look.

"You can sleep with me, only for tonight. Just because I'm letting you sleep with me for tonight doesn't mean your ass still isn't in the doghouse."

"I know." I smiled like a little kid, climbing in next to her. I was tired of sleeping on the damn couch, and the back pain was becoming unbearable. I snuggled Celeste in my arms, feeling the warmth I've been missing.

"Hey, can I ask you something?"

"Wassup?" I asked, closing my eyes.

"Do you know a guy named Reggie?" When that sentence left her mouth, I felt as if I were about to shit bricks. I didn't know what the hell Reggie told her, and for her to ask me if I knew him didn't sit right with me.

"No, why?"

"No reason, he just looks familiar. I could have sworn I've seen him in the streets of New York. I signed a copy of my book for him, and he was telling me about him and his boyfriend wanting to try new things."

I swallowed the lump in my throat, trying to find a topic to change the subject with. I made a mental note in my head to fuck Reggie up the next time I saw him.

"Oh."

"Yeah, I never knew I had readers in the LGBTQ community. I've been debating on branching out and writing about my main characters being gay and lesbian."

"Oh, okay, that's good, baby. Look, I'm tired, so I'm about to go to sleep," I replied, getting uncomfortable hearing her talk about this. She sighed and said okay before turning the TV off and going to sleep. The entire time I was up, I curious about what the hell Reggie told her.

Chapter 18: Stalking Ain't Easy

One Month Later

But you didn't have to cut me off
Make out like it never happened and that we were nothing
And I don't even need your love
But you treat me like a stranger and that feels so rough
~Gotye

Seeing Celeste and her husband at the event in Seattle threw me off. I've seen her at plenty of events before, and he had never been at any of them. It was always her sister with her. Him being with her threw me off. I just knew he would recognize me from the club that night. That lets me know he doesn't pay attention to his surroundings. It's no way in hell I wouldn't remember the face of a man I saw my wife snatch away from. Him not asking questions let me know he didn't pay attention to her as much as he should.

After the event, I continued to call and e-mail Celeste every day, hoping she would answer me, but she didn't. Most guys would have given up, but I wasn't one of them. Instead, I took another route. I decided to sit outside the bookstore that Celeste's sister owned, hoping that she would come by there. The plan was to see her and follow her home so that I could see where she lived. I sat outside that store damn near a week before Celeste came to the store.

On that particular day, she seemed to be picking her sister up for a girl's day out. Their first stop was a spa. I grew up with two sisters, so I knew once they went in there, they would be there for hours. To pass the time, I went around the corner to a local restaurant and grabbed a cheeseburger, some fries, and a Coke to go for me to eat while I waited outside the spa. I had been so busy putting my master plan together, that I skipped breakfast and was starving.

After getting my food, I drove back to the spa to start my wait process. While I was eating, I couldn't help but think about the time I had Celeste pussy in my mouth. The taste of it was one that I would savor forever. I hoped that soon, I could have it in my mouth again. Once I finished my food, I opened my laptop to work on some things for the book club.

∞∞∞

Two hours later, Celeste and her sister emerged from the spa looking refreshed. They went to the same restaurant I had gotten my food from. Now, I was mentally kicking myself for not waiting to see if they would get food before I ate. Thankfully, I had a hat in the car that I could pull down over my face as a disguise to go inside. Typically, I took my hats off indoors, but this wasn't a normal situation. I asked the hostess to sit me at a table near Celeste and her sister. I sat with my back turned to them so that I could hear better, and my face couldn't be seen. I ordered a salad and a lava cake even though I was full. It would be something for me to have for dinner or breakfast the next morning.

After the waitress took my order, I leaned back a little so that I could hear the conversation Celeste was having with her sister.

"Thanks for making time for me, sis. I feel like we have only been communicating in passing lately."

"No need to thank me. You've been busy lately, which is a good thing. When do you leave for California?"

"Tomorrow morning. Mom is picking the twins up tonight and keeping them until I get back. Kadarius will check in with them from time to time while I'm gone."

"Speaking of Kadarius, how's it going with him being back in the house?"

"Not bad, actually. I still haven't let him back in our bedroom, but it's nice to be under the same roof. The kids are starting to be receptive to him again. Well, Cassie is, KJ is still on the fence."

"KJ will come around. What about your relationship with him?"

"I'm taking it one day at a time."

Their food came, and they chit-chatted about random things while they ate. When I heard them ask for the check, I told the waitress I had an emergency and had to leave. I gave her a fifty-dollar bill and told her to keep the change. Shortly after I was in my car, the women came out. Celeste dropped her sister back off at her store and headed back home.

To my surprise, she lived out in Manhattan near the hotel we spent that incredible evening at. I parked across the street where she wouldn't notice me, took a picture of the house so I wouldn't forget which one it was, and drove off.

The next morning, I was back across the street from Celeste's house bright and early so that I could start on my plans for the day. A cab pulled up to the house, and Celeste came out with her husband behind her helping with her bags. This guy was making wrong moves all around. Had she been my wife, I would have driven her to the airport myself. He loaded her bags in the trunk, kissed her goodbye, and then went back inside the house. About twenty minutes later, Kadarius came back out in a brown and white pinstripe suit and matching shoes. I wasn't close enough to guess the designer, but it looked expensive. Once he was gone, I waited about thirty minutes to make sure he wasn't coming back before getting out.

I walked around the house checking for an easy way in and got lucky when I found a window cracked open. When I pushed it up, I expected an alarm to go off that I would have to disarm, but to my surprise, there was silence. That means they didn't have one or his dumb ass forgot to arm it.

Not wanting to waste any time, I quickly pulled out my indoor Mobotix C26 cameras and began planting them throughout the house. I put one in the kitchen, the living room, the master bedroom, and the basement area. Once I was done, I went back to my car and opened my laptop to make sure the cameras were working. After finding out they were, I pulled off.

∞ ∞ ∞

I spent the rest of my day taking calls and checking e-mails. Around five in the evening, I got an alert on my laptop that there was movement in Celeste's house. I figured it was just her husband returning home. When I looked at the cameras, I noticed he wasn't alone. He and this mystery person appeared to be in a heated argument. It was times like this I wished I had opted for the cameras with sound so that I could hear what they were saying.

I watched them get in each other's faces for what seemed like forever before calming down. I thought once the argument was done, the person would leave, but they didn't. What took place next shocked me so much that I had to rub my eyes to make sure it wasn't a dream.

"Well, I'll be damned," I voiced aloud to myself before

closing the computer.

Chapter 19: Gut Feeling

Celeste

Looking in your eyes, I been feeling like I'm crazy
Cause I'm going through your phone, look
for something wrong, I can't find nothing
I must be tripping tryna listen to my intuition, say you guilty
So baby, just tell me, I never asked before, but
right now I don't know what's going on
~H.E.R, Ella Mai

Laurel, Angela, Charlotte, and I were sitting on our private plane ride to California, which was sent out by the team of directors and producers who were working on my movie. Jolani would have come, but I knew she didn't have time to take off of work, and she even offered to help Kadarius out with the kids for the time being that I was gone. As bad as I didn't want to travel back and forth to work on this film due to me having to leave the kids behind, it was a dream of mine that I wanted to make come true.

"Why are you so nervous?" Laurel asked, nudging my shoulder.

"I don't know. I just miss the kids already, and I'm so stuck in my work that I forgot how it feels to travel and be out of New York."

"Well, that's a sign that you need to take more vacations, hun," Charlotte chimed in, taking a sip of her mimosa.

"You can say that again."

"So, Kadarius?" Laurel asked.

"What about him?"

"What the hell are you two doing? Are y'all together, or are y'all not together? What's going on?"

"We're working through our issues."

"Oh lord, I don't know why you won't just drop his ass. You know I never liked him, even back then when you two first got together, something was always off about his ass." Charlotte disclosed.

"You don't like nobody."

"Okay and, I understand the two of you have kids, but I know when my sister isn't happy, and you're not happy. You need some new dick in your life."

"Shut your ass up. I'm fine with fixing things in my marriage."

"Okay, Kirk and Rasheeda."

"Okay, now you getting disrespectful, heffa."

"I'm just saying, can you not handle the truth, Rasheeda?"

"Stop calling me that, and he isn't cheating on me."

"How you know? His ass probably got bitches all throughout Manhattan while you're home playing the innocent, respectful, wife."

"Angela?" I asked, wanting to get her thoughts.

"I gotta side with Charlotte on this one," she replied, throwing her hands up in surrender.

"Are y'all serious right now?" I scoffed in disbelief.

"Yeah, I mean, my ex cheated on me multiple times, and from what you told me, it sounds just like that. I understand patching things up for the kids but don't act as if you don't get the slightest feeling that he's sneaking around on you," Angela spoke out.

I sighed and leaned back in my seat, thinking about what my sisters were telling me. Shit was slowly getting back to normal between us, and now that I was miles away from home, the thought of him cheating was heavy on my mind.

"Fix your face. You're about to have your book turned into a movie. Don't worry about him, right now this is all about you," Charlotte ordered, passing me a glass, and pouring me some Chardonnay. I smiled, seeing that she remembered it was my favorite.

"You're right."

"I know I'm right. Hey, we meant to ask you about the guy from the club."

"What guy?" I asked, playing dumb.

"The dude you were about to throw the pussy too."

"I wasn't about to throw my pussy at nobody. You need a filter on your mouth."

"Girl please, I would throw my pussy on him. That's one fine ass man. His name was Raymon, right?" she asked.

Just hearing his name, I swallowed the lump in my throat and cleared it. The last thing I needed was my sister going after him, for him to find an easier way to get to me. It seemed as if the more I rejected him, the stronger he came onto me, and it was creeping me out. I didn't like to blame others in situations because I partially blame myself for letting things get this far. Instead of thinking with my head and my many degrees, I was thinking with my girl downstairs, and she got us in a fucked-up position. Shit was so weird around Raymon that every time I saw him or thought of him, it made me feel ambivalent.

Once we touched down in California, we got off the plane

and made our way to our hotel. After a five-hour flight, I wanted to lie down and stay in motion. Charlotte, Laurel, and Angela decided to spend some time at the bar downstairs, while I stayed in the room. Sighing and grabbing my MacBook, I opened it and opened up a new doc to write a new story.

"*Gut Feelings 2: Out For Blood*, by C.K. Norwood," I said aloud, typing the title.

Gut Feeling was a story I wrote back in my DreamPen days. After publishing the first book, I left my readers with a cliffhanger. I lost inspiration for the story a while back, but after receiving this movie deal, motivation was taking me over by the second. *Gut Feeling* was a story about a girl who was a famous porn star, and she met a guy who she thought loved her for her and not her background. In reality, he wanted her for being a porn star and the fame, and when she found out his games, she dropped him and started a family with another man, along with finding a new job. The guy then stalked her and make her life hell. The stalker then kidnaps the main female lead, and my readers assumed she was dead. I knew Christmas was coming up and releasing this book with a basket full of my merch would have been the perfect present for my readers over the holidays.

Picking up my phone, I called Kadarius to ask him how things were, but he didn't answer. His not answering was just making my gut feeling worse than before. The talk on the plane already had my nerves on ten thousand, and him not answering me didn't help the case. It wasn't like him not to answer my calls while I was out of town, and I was curious about what had him occupied.

As soon as I was about to start typing, I rolled my eyes seeing an e-mail from someone anonymous pop up in my notifications. Hesitant to open it, I sighed and clicked it anyway. As soon as I opened the e-mail, I read it aloud.

"From your biggest fan, a queen like you should know what's going on in your kingdom."

I raised my eyebrow in suspicion at a link he sent me. Praying that it wasn't something out of pocket, I clicked the link, and a live video began to play.

Chapter 20: Shame

Kadarius

"Shit, right there," I moaned, pushing Reggie's head down further.

The only sounds that could be heard throughout my home were the sounds of Reggie slurping and sucking me up. After Celeste left to catch her plane, I had to get ready to pick the kids up from camp. In the midst of me trying to head out, as soon as I opened the door, Reggie was standing there distraught. Due to our history with one another, I couldn't turn him around without finding out why he was depressed or upset. As pissed off as I was about him showing up to my place unannounced, I couldn't leave him out in the rain when he needed me. When he told how me he was losing his firm, I felt sorry for him because I knew how much work it took to put in to get where we are. I worked my ass off to get my firm, and to lose it like it was nothing could be the worst nightmare anyone could ask for. A simple venting session then turned into something more within minutes.

I licked my lips and tilted my head back as he rubbed his hands down my chest, while humming, causing vibrations on my dick. Once I felt myself cumming, I tried to pull him off of me, but he pushed my hand away, letting me cum in his mouth. I gripped the black satin sheets, as I released my warm nut into his mouth. Catching my breath, I looked down at him as he watched me with seductive eyes, swallowing every drop.

Reggie then got off of his knees before stroking me and massaging my balls. Once I heard my phone ring for the fifth time, I tried to push Reggie off so that I could grab it, but he wouldn't let me.

"It's supposed to be our moment. I don't give a damn if the Obama's was ranging your line. I'm focusing on you, and you need to focus on me."

"It might be important, chill."

"It's not important. I'm telling you that now, before you ruin the moment by answering that phone."

"I'm not ruining shit. You need to chill with all this possessive shit," I replied, standing up, making him stop.

"Or what? You gonna drop me?"

"If it comes to that, I just might."

"Hmm, and I might tell your wife," he mumbled.

I snatched my neck around so hard that it was liable to come off my shoulders. I walked up on him, pushing him into the wall. Once he saw the seriousness in my face, he gave me a like, daring to test me.

"What I tell you about that shit? I don't wanna hear my wife name roll off your tongue ever again, you hear me?"

"Get out of my face."

"I said do you fucking hear me!" I yelled, punching the wall behind him that was inches away from his head.

"What are we, KD?" Reggie quizzed, shaking his head.

"I'm not having this conversation with you, Reg. I said what I said. Keep my wife out of what we have."

"What do we have?"

"It's about to be nothing."

"Did you think about my offer?"

"What offer?"

"What we talked about back at my place." He sighed.

"I'm not leaving my wife and my kids to move with you to another state."

"You said you were going to last time."

"We were both off the Henny. You know I didn't mean that."

"Whatever, bye, Kadarius. I'm tired of kissing your ass to try to stick with me."

"Okay, get stepping," I replied, moving to the side so he could leave.

"I will, this new nigga I'm fucking with wouldn't treat me like this," Reggie disclosed, grabbing his clothes from the floor, catching me off guard.

"New nigga, huh?" I laughed to myself.

"Yeah, we met at the bar last month. He'll appreciate me more than you do."

Just hearing the thought of somebody else stealing Reggie's time from me had me hot. I walked over to him and grabbed his arm.

"You gonna stop playing with me," I warned through gritted teeth.

"Or what?" he quipped, getting in my face.

I pushed him on the bed, making him fall on his back, before climbing on top of him.

"So, you giving away what's mine?"

"You don't want me, remember."

"Fuck you!" I spat, hating that he was right.

"Okay, fuck me then," he challenged, turning around to lie on his stomach.

I just sat there, staring at Reggie. How smooth his chocolate complexion was, how dominant yet submissive he was. Deciding not to pass up that chance, I licked my lips and slapped his ass, preparing myself to put in work. We went at it for a good two hours in the bedroom and then we migrated to my man cave before falling asleep.

∞ ∞ ∞

Loud knocks on the front door awoke me. Panic automatically rushed through my body like lightning, thinking the worst. Shit, whoever it was at the door, had my heart beating out of my chest. I rushed and put my clothes on before trying to frantically wake Reggie up.

"Wake up!" I semi-yelled.

"What? Why?"

"Somebody's at the door. You gotta go."

"Just go get the door and tell them to leave."

"Reggie, you gotta go now."

He sighed before letting out a mighty yawn and getting out of bed to get dressed. I ran out of my room, and as soon as I was about to open the door for whoever it was, the door swung open on its own. I cursed to myself upon seeing the twins walk through the doors drenched.

Shit, I forgot I had to pick the twins up. I cursed myself.

When I saw Celeste's best friend Jolani walk through the doors, I felt as if I were about to hyperventilate. I rushed down the stairs and tried to appear to her as normal as possible.

"So, you forgot you had kids?" she voiced with her arms

crossed.

"It slipped my mind."

"Your kids slipped your mind?" she asked, with a raised eyebrow.

"I had a lot going on," I lied.

"Fuck that explanation shit to me. You better prepare yourself for what your wife gotta say to you about this."

"You told her?"

"No, the camp called her since you weren't picking up. Celeste wasn't picking up either, so they called me as another emergency contact. I'm not mad at her for not answering because she's working, but you're supposed to be off watching your kids. What the hell is going on with you?" Jolani ranted.

"A lot."

"Kadarius, save that bullshit for someone else. Next time make your kids your first priority."

"How did you get in?"

"Celeste gave the twins a key before leaving this morning."

"Oh, well, thank you for picking them up."

"Mhm, whatever don't let it happen again. Got my damn god kids waiting in the rain for you."

I watched as she hugged the twins and walked out of the house. The kids didn't even look at me. They just stripped out of their wet coats and went to the kitchen to eat. I knew they were pissed with me because I left them out in the rain for hours, now I was feeling like shit for what I pulled. I would have hoped Reggie found a way out because the last thing I needed was the twins seeing him. I went into the kitchen and saw them pulling McDonald bags from their backpack.

"How was camp?" I asked them.

"How do you think it went?" Cassie sassed, rolling her eyes. She had the same angry expression Celeste held when she was pissed, and I knew she was about to give it to me. She had a smart mouth, just like her mother.

"I'm sorry."

"No, you're not," KJ mumbled, popping a fry in his mouth.

"I am, I just got busy an—"

"Let me guess, work. You always work. It's always work. It's like you don't even love us anymore," Cassie remarked, pushing her food away and looking at me with her arms crossed.

I tucked my lips in, looking at my daughter doing nothing but accepting the jab to the chest.

"I promise I'm gonna do better. how about I take you two out to eat?"

"I'm okay. I'm not even hungry anymore." Cassie pouted, walking off toward her bedroom. I looked over at KJ, and he just shook his head before following his sister. Cassie was technically the oldest by a few minutes, and you could tell by the way KJ followed behind her.

I leaned on the wall and sighed, hearing the room doors slam. I couldn't even find it in me to yell at her or sternly discipline her because she was right. Once I saw Reggie sneaking down the stairs, he gave me an apologetic look, not saying anything, just walking out, leaving me alone with my shame.

Chapter 21: Masking the Pain

Celeste

If he ain't gonna love you the way he should

Then let it go

~Keyshia Cole

"On behalf of S & S Films and Author C.K. Norwood, I would like to thank you all for coming to the auditions today. We have all of your information and will reach out to you soon," the director said to the actors and actresses.

"Yes, thank you all so much," I added.

Once they all walked out, we discussed the ones that I liked for the movie. There were some people I felt were perfect, and I hoped the director agreed with me. We talked for about an hour before we left. I had to meet with them about a few things tomorrow, and then I was headed back home.

Laurel, Charlotte, and Angela were out sightseeing. I was supposed to meet up with them, but I was drained. Not only was this movie a lot of work, but the things that I had to deal with when I got home were on my mind. Besides, those three could always sense when something was wrong with me, and there was no way in hell, I could explain this. Thank God they weren't around when I viewed that horrific video.

I got back to my hotel room, stripped out of my clothes, and got in the shower. A hot bath was what I needed to hide my tears. This was the first time I had been able to cry since I saw that video. There were so many emotions running through me, but the humiliation was the dominant one. Most people would assume hurt. However, that wasn't the case.

Truth be told, I've been suspecting Kadarius of cheating for some time now. We barely have sex, he's never home, and when he "works" late, he doesn't answer his phone. As an attorney, I get that he has a lot of work to do and is busy. That's no excuse for not checking on your wife and kids. Anything could happen to us, and he wouldn't know it until he decided to go home. We had plenty of arguments about it, but after countless lies about him fixing it, I let it go.

When I thought about him cheating, I often wondered what the woman looked like. Was her ass fatter than mine? Did she have big breasts? Was her head game on point? Now knowing the truth, I found myself asking a different set of questions. How long has he liked men? Have there been multiple men or just this one? What was this man doing that I couldn't? More importantly, why did he think it was okay to bring this man into our house?

Once my water started getting cold, I got out of the shower, threw on some pajamas, and laid across the bed. My stomach growled, reminding me it had been a few hours since I ate something. I didn't want to leave the room, so I ordered room service. After doing that, I text the girls, letting them know I was in for the evening. I knew once they got back to the hotel, they would come looking for me. It was times like this I was so thankful that I had my own room.

I called the kids on FaceTime to check on them once the ladies text me back, letting me know they would see me tomorrow afternoon when we got ready to leave.

"Mommy!" Cassie screamed when she answered.

"Hey, baby! How are you? Where's your brother?"

KJ leaned in where I could see him.

"Hey, mom!"

"Hey, big man! How are you guys? Are you having fun with your dad?"

The smiles on their faces immediately fell at the mention of their father letting me know something was wrong. Before I could ask what happened, Cassie spoke up.

"Mom, the next time you go out of town, can you leave us with grandma instead of dad?"

"Why? Did something happen?"

"You didn't see the calls from our camp director?"

"I did, but it was late. I called your dad that night, and he told me everything was fine."

"Well, he lied," KJ voiced with an attitude.

Normally I wouldn't have allowed him to call his father a liar, but he clearly had a reason to.

"What happened?" I asked again.

Cassie explained how he never picked them up from camp that day. That they stood out in the rain for at least an hour before they got picked up. When I asked why they weren't inside, she told me the director had the building locked and wasn't aware they were out there.

"If he didn't pick you up, how did you guys get home?"

"Aunt Jojo picked us up. Before you ask, no dad wasn't at work. He was home when we got here. He told Jojo he forgot about us. My throat has been hurting since then," Cassie explained.

"Yea, mine too," KJ added.

I told them I would be home tomorrow to take them to the doctor. I was sure they didn't tell their father they weren't feeling well.

"In the meantime, I'm gonna have Jojo bring you guys

some chicken noodle soup. That will help until I get there."

"Thanks, mom!" they said in unison.

I talked to them for a few more minutes before hanging up. Just when I thought I couldn't cry anymore, the tears started flowing again. Not only was he fucking another man, but he had also chosen him over his kids.

Chapter 22: When Secrets Surface

Kadarius

The Next Night

How long will it be
Before you treat her like your queen?
And how long will it take
Before she starts coming home too late?
And how long will it be
Before she starts running in the streets?
You better take the time to treat her like your lady.
~Joe

I sang along to Joe's hit record "Treat Her Like A Lady" while I cooked dinner for Celeste and me I. The twins were with Jolani for the evening so we could spend some much-needed alone time together. Almost getting caught with Reggie in the house scared me shitless and put a lot of things in perspective for me. Fucking with Reggie wasn't pleasurable anymore. Well, let me rephrase that because the sex is beyond pleasurable. However, he doesn't understand his place anymore. When we first started messing around, he understood that I had a family, and being with him was my escape. I'll admit that I caught feelings and slightly entertained the idea of being with him permanently, but his actions changed that. Had he continued to go with the flow like we're doing, things would be different.

I knew Jolani was going to run her mouth to Celeste about me forgetting to pick up the kids from camp, so I had to do something to calm her before she found out. I sent her a text asking what time she wanted me to pick her up from the airport. When she told me that she didn't need a ride, I decided to cook a romantic dinner for us. I had gone all out. Lobster tails, crab legs, and shrimp were all on the menu, which were her favorites. I also had a bottle of her favorite wine chilling. Once we were done with dinner, I planned to run her a hot bubble bath and bathe her. I used to do things like this all the time when we first got married. It's about time I started back.

I heard the door open as I was finishing up the food.

"Welcome home, baby!" I greeted Celeste.

"What's all this?" she asked me.

"I decided to make dinner. Come sit down while I fix our plates."

Reluctantly, she put her bags down and sat down at the table. I assumed she was tired, and that's where her resistance was coming from. After fixing the plates, I sat them at the table then went back into the kitchen to get the wine.

"Oh, wow! You went all out. I forgot you know how to cook like this," Celeste said with an attitude.

"Funny, but I deserve that," I commented when I returned.

We said our grace and dug in. Well, I did. Celeste was pushing her food around her plate.

"Are you not hungry?"

"So, did anything happen while I was away that I need to be aware of?"

Celeste asking me this let me know that Jolani had run her mouth already. I explained to her that I was tired when I got off and accidentally fell asleep.

"I know you depended on me while you were away, baby. I apologize, and it won't happen again."

"You were sleep, huh?"

"Yes, sweetheart. This case that I've been working on has

been draining me."

She looked at me as if she didn't believe a word I was saying. I was about to ask her why she didn't, but she beat me to the punch.

"So, if you were at home sleeping, then who is this in this video?

She handed me her phone, and I almost pissed myself when I saw what was on the screen. There I was on camera getting my dick sucked by Reggie. As a lawyer, I could talk my way out of a lot of things, but this wasn't one of them.

"How did you get this? Wait… you've been spying on me?"

"How I got it should be the least of your worries. To answer your question, no, I haven't been spying on you. This was sent to me in an anonymous e-mail."

I should have known Celeste would never go as far as planting cameras to catch me doing something. That wasn't her style. Without saying anything else, I got up and went down to my man cave with Celeste on my tail. From the angle of the video, I was able to tell exactly where the camera was.

"There's no telling how long this has been here," I said.

"Do you think there are some in the rest of the house?"

We went from room to room, searching for more cameras. We found them in our bedroom and the living room. Thankfully, none were in the kids' room.

"We need to be more alert until we find out what's going on," I said to Celeste.

"The fuck you mean *we*? Oh, so you thought these hidden cameras would make me forget you were fucking another man in our house, huh? Hell no! How long have you been with him? Were there others before him?"

"Baby, please don't do this."

"Answer the questions, Kadarius!" Celeste yelled.

"It's been going on a while, and no, there weren't any men before. I fucked up, and it will never happen again."

"Oh, I know it won't happen again because I'm done. You can live in your man cave until I figure out a way to explain this to the kids, but our marriage is over."

"Over? You can't be serious? Baby, we can fix this."

"Had it been a woman, then fixing it might have been an option, but you been fucking a whole man!"

"What difference does it make?"

"You can't be serious! There are a lot of things a woman can tolerate, but knowing her husband is fucking another man isn't one of them. What did I do that was so bad that you ran into the arms of another man?"

I felt like shit after hearing her ask me that. I told her there was nothing wrong with her. She had been the perfect wife. Looking in her eyes, I could tell she didn't believe me, but it was the truth. Rather than go back and forth with her, I told her I would give her some space. I walked back to my man cave, feeling terrible. I kept telling myself I would start doing right by my wife, and now it was too late.

While I was laying down, tears formed in my eyes. I was sad about losing my wife and angry that somebody had the audacity to put cameras in our house. I racked my brain trying to figure out who would do this shit, then it hit me. Reggie!

Chapter 23: Creep

Raymon

I sat in my chair, looking down at my laptop, watching the rush of panic fill Kadarius and Celeste's face. Once they found the cameras, it made me feel agitated that I couldn't monitor the inside. I was still yet relieved that Celeste received my e-mail. Shit, if I was disgusted as a man, I knew she was sickened as a woman, seeing her husband getting top from another man. My cameras weren't there to catch her man in the act. They were there to keep an eye on her. I guess this was a plus because I saw everything that went down before they deactivated my cameras. I did nothing but smile at how everything was falling into place. Cutting my laptop off, I pulled my phone from my pocket, seeing I got a text from Jolani.

Since I felt as if I was at a standstill with getting closer to Celeste, I felt as if I needed to take drastic measures. Due to a little research, I ran across Celeste's best friend, Jolani Harris. Since it seemed like they were always around one another, I decided to pursue her and to try to get closer to her. After replying to her invitation to come over to her place, I grabbed my jacket and my keys, heading out to my car. Getting inside my car, I turned my radio up, pulling out of the driveway.

∞∞∞

It took me a good hour to get to Jolani's spot. When I arrived, I pulled up beside her 2018 silver Acura. Getting out of the car, I locked my doors and made my way to the front door. Knocking twice, within seconds, I heard the locks click, and the door swung open, revealing Jolani. Her light skin complexion shimmered like diamonds, and she sported a different hair color from our last time meeting.

"Hey." She smiled, pushing her red Peruvian bundles behind her ear.

"Wassup, baby girl?" I smiled, looking down at her. She was in nothing but a pair of Nike sports shorts and a white tank top. By the looks of her nipples on hard poking through her shirt, I could tell she wasn't wearing a bra.

"Nothing much, I just needed someone to talk to. I know we're hitting things off slow, but there's still so much that I haven't learned about you."

"So, you thought tonight would be perfect for twenty-one questions?" I quizzed sarcastically.

"You told me to text you whenever I was ready to meet with you again, so tonight I'm ready. If it's an issue, you can go."

"It's no issue at all." I smirked, eyeing her down. Even though she was petite, Jolani was curvy in the waist area, had a little ass, and she kind of had a bird chest, but her beauty in the face made up for the negatives.

"Great," she replied, waving for me to come in.

Once I walked in, I looked around at her decor as I did, the last two times I've been here. It was simple but unique in many ways. It was a light shade of blue, white, and gray, which complimented each other. Once I saw toys on the floor, I looked over at her, wondering if her ass had kids and didn't tell me.

"Oh, excuse the mess. Those are my niece and nephew's toys. I just put them to sleep not long ago," she disclosed while rushing over to the toys and putting them in a toy bin.

Once the blue leather couch was clear, I took a seat and admired the family photos on the wall. The picture of Celeste and Jolani that hung over the fireplace drew my attention in. It was a photo of both the women at the beach, throwing up peace signs and making funny faces.

"That's my best friend," Jolani revealed, taking a seat near me, bringing her attention to the photo I was staring at.

"C.K Norwood is your best friend? Wow, that's crazy, she's a beast with that pen," I said playing clueless, knowing it would give me brownie points.

"Yes, she is. That girl is like my sister. You a fan of her work?"

"At this point, I'm *past being a fan.*"

"Wow, well, maybe one day I could get you to meet her."

"We've met before, we're well acquainted with one another."

"Oh really, how so?"

"I've been following her work for a minute, and I've been to meet and greets and everything."

"Hmm, well on her behalf, thank you for the support."

"It's nothing."

"But hey, I have beer in the fridge if you'd like one. Or if you want some wine, I have a few bottles."

"You got Bud Light?"

"Yeah, give me just a minute."

I nodded and made sure she was out of sight before taking a photo of the photo on the fireplace of Celeste and Jolani. When I heard footsteps, I turned around to see a little girl instead of Jolani. I smiled, seeing how much she looked like Celeste. Her features were strong.

"Hey." I waved at her.

"My mama said not to talk to strangers," she replied, pulling her blanket over her shoulders. Looking at the clock on the wall, I saw it was after midnight.

"I'm not a stranger, I know your mother." I smiled, standing up and walking over to her but she stepped back, looking up at me.

"Who's my mama then?" she sassed.

"Celeste Norwood." She was hesitant at first before sighing.

"Okay, who are you?"

"I'm Raymon, a close friend of your moms."

"I've never seen you before."

"I work a lot. What's your name?" I smirked, kneeling down, eyeing her up and down. She shared Celeste's same skin complexion, her hair was curly and hung to her mid back, and she had the same eyes that her mother sucked me in with.

"I'm Cassie."

"I like that name, Cassie. You're very beautiful." I smiled, caressing her cheek.

"Thank you." she replied, stepping back so I wouldn't touch her face again. I even noticed the slight discomfort on her face.

"So how old are you, Cassie?"

"Six."

"Wow, you don't even look six. You're a beautiful big girl. I bet you get that a lot."

"Yeah." Cassie fake smiled.

"Do you like ice cream?"

"Yeah."

"Maybe one day you and I can go get some ice cream,

would you like that?" I asked, grabbing her hand, caressing the top of her small soft hands with my thumb.

"Yeah, if my brother KJ can come, and my mama and daddy."

"What if I want it to be only me and you?"

"I don't like that."

"Why?"

"Because I don't know you."

"That's why we would get ice cream so you can get to know me."

"I'll think about it."

"Okay, why are you up so late?"

"I can't sleep."

"Why?"

"I don't know. I just can't sleep."

"You wanna know a trick?"

"Yeah." She smiled, showing her straight pearly whites.

"I count sheep to go to sleep."

"Counting sheep? Why?"

"You can count something other than sheep. You should try it."

"Okay, I will. Goodnight," Cassie replied, trying to walk off but I grabbed her arm, making her jump and turn to me with fear in her face.

I knew fear when I saw it, and for some reason that emotion turned me on. I enjoyed feeling like the dominant one and I loved a hint of fear in a woman's face because I knew I had the upper hand.

"No hug?" I pouted.

"Can you let me go?"

"I'll let you go, when I get a hug." I smiled.

She was hesitant but wrapped her arms around my neck and I embraced her, inhaling the scent of Johnson & Johnson's vanilla scented baby lotion. I traced my hands from her upper back, before caressing her butt. She gasped and pushed me before running off toward her room. As soon as I got off of my knee, I turned around to see Jolani coming back from the kitchen with my beer, and a glass of wine for herself.

"Thank you." I smiled, taking the beer from her.

"Your welcome."

"Look, I smoked a joint before I came over here, so I'm buzzed. And seeing you earlier wearing this, got me hard."

"Oh wow, so?"

"So, you gonna fix what you started?" I smirked, knowing she wouldn't turn me down.

I learned that Jolani was the easy type for men. She was hurt by so many men that she let them use her and I saw that as an advantage for me. She smirked before downing her wine and grabbing my hand, guiding me to her bedroom. In all actuality, it wasn't even her that got me on hard, it was Cassie.

I felt that switch in my head go off and I already knew I wasn't going to be myself anymore. The thought of Cassie's tiny hands caressing my chest and kissing me ran through my mind as Jolani sucked me off in her bedroom. Shit, I felt like a creep, a weirdo, but who was gonna stop me, no fucking body. If I couldn't imagine having my way with Celeste, imagining it with her daughter would have to do. I knew for a fact if I imagined Celeste sucking my dick, I was liable to call her name out, but I knew for a fact it would have been a different story with Cassie.

Chapter 24: Dirty Laundry

Let's do this dirty laundry, this dirty laundry
When you're soaked in tears for years, it never airs out
When you make pain look this good it never wears out
This dirty laundry, this dirty laundry
~Kelly Rowland

Two Months Later

"Cassie, KJ come on!" I yelled, fishing for my keys in my pocket.

They were staying at Kadarius' new place this weekend and in the process, I was still trying to get all of his belongings out of the house. After the night we found the cameras in our house, I was pretty spooked out. So, spooked out that the cameras were the only thing that distracted me from busting Kadarius' ass upside his head with the wine bottle he had in the middle of the table. Even after finding the cameras and destroying them, I was still on edge feeling as if I was being watched. Kadarius was as oblivious as I was with finding out where the cameras came from. After that night, I stayed in a nearby hotel because I wasn't ready to stay in a house with Kadarius. I was liable to smother him in his sleep for pulling what he pulled.

He pleaded with me almost every second of the day for me to forgive him, but forgiveness was something that I couldn't give him. He had the nerve to fuck another man in our house, the house that we conceived out twins in, the house that we made love in. He fucked another man in my home and wanted me to dust that shit to the side like it was cookies and creme. I was still livid just thinking about it.

Once he got the hint that I wanted a divorce and that I was serious, we sat the kids down and broke the news to them. They asked plenty of questions, most questions I couldn't even answer. KJ took it hard because he loved being around both of us. Cassie was more so confused and worried. We knew the divorce would affect our kids one way or another, but I couldn't stay in a broken marriage and pretend like I was happy in front of my kids. Kadarius rented a cheap but nice apartment on the other side of town, not too far from the kids, and they spent the weekends with him.

KJ came downstairs with his Fortnite bookbag clinging off his shoulders, with his iPad in his hand.

"Where's Cassie?" I asked, seeing she wasn't behind him. I noticed she was a little distant lately, and she rarely talked. As bad as I didn't want to blame myself for this, I was doing that. I knew this divorce was taking a toll on her.

"She's in her room."

"Why is she in her room? I told her we were leaving."

"I don't know." He shrugged.

I sighed before making my way upstairs to her bedroom. I knocked twice before opening her door to see her sitting at the head of her bed with her knees tucked to her chest. Walking over, I sat on her bed and placed my hand on her leg, making her jump.

"What's wrong?" I asked, noticing that she had been crying.

"I don't wanna talk about it."

"You sure? You know I'm always here to listen to you. Remember we never keep secrets."

"I don't wanna talk about it." she repeated, sniffling. I assumed she was emotional about the divorce so instead of talking it out with her while she was emotional, I postponed the conversation for another day.

"Are you ready to go to your dad's?"

"No, can I stay with you."

"Why don't you wanna go to dad's?"

"I wanna stay with you," she replied, climbing over to me. For a six-year-old, Cassie was big, and I still climbed in my lap as if she was a toddler. I smiled and hugged her in my arms before planting a kiss on her forehead.

"Okay, you can stay with me. Let's go drop your brother off."

She nodded before getting out of my lap and going downstairs to meet with her brother. I followed them downstairs, and they got in the car. After setting my alarm and my personal cameras outside of my house, I went to the car and pulled out of the driveway.

∞ ∞ ∞

It didn't take long before I arrived at Kadarius place. I walked KJ to the front of his door before knocking. Kadarius opened the door and knelt down, smiling in excitement seeing KJ.

"Hey, missed you. You ready to stay the weekend with me?" He smiled, pulling KJ into a hug.

"Yeah." KJ cheesed in excitement. KJ ran into the house leaving Kadarius and I alone at the door.

"Where's Cassie?" he asked.

"She wanted to stay with me, so I'm letting her."

"She good?"

"Yeah she's fine, just still coping with this."

"So am I." Kadarius frowned, massaging his beard.

"Too bad."

"I miss you too. I miss us."

"Hmm, would have thought you would have missed letting another man suck your dick in our bedroom."

"I deserve that."

"Oh, nigga you deserve more than that, let's change the subject before I beat your ass in front of these kids," I replied, feeling my blood boil.

"We're going to have to talk about this sooner or later."

"I guess it'll be later."

"Somebody has to be the mature one."

"I said we'd talk about it later."

"Okay, I respect that."

"You have no choice but to respect it, look I gotta go. I'll pick him up Monday from school."

"Thank you."

"Mhm, and next month I'm going back to California to finish up this movie deal, so the kids can either stay with you, Jolani, or I can drop them off to my mother."

"They can stay with me."

"Okay," I replied, trying to walk off, but he grabbed me.

"I'm proud of you."

"Boy fuck you, go watch my child," I sassed, rolling my eyes, heading back to my car.

I pulled out of the driveway and made my way to the laundromat. Since my dryer was broken, I went to the laundromat on Jolani's side of town so that I could sit and talk with her. I felt as if I haven't spoken to her in a while.

"Cassie, what do you want to eat later?" I asked, sparking up a conversation noticing that she was staring off into space.

"I don't know." she shrugged.

"How about this, we can go to the movies after we leave here, go get some Chinese food, and then go to the spa?"

"Really?" She smiled, looking over at me.

"Yes, really, you wanna do that?"

"Yeah." She cheesed in excitement.

I smiled at how excited she was before finding a parking spot. I grabbed the bag full of clothes with Cassie right on my trail. In the midst of going through the clothes to put in each washer, I noticed Kadarius' old football jersey. I traced my hands across the big number one on the front of the turquoise jersey. I suddenly smiled, remembering the night he asked me to be his girlfriend in the same jersey.

"Girl, if you don't jump on him, I will," Angela commented, pointing to the school's star quarterback, Kadarius Norwood.

"That boy does not want me. He's probably got hoes all over this damn school. I know you hear how these females be talking about him. If he got devil dick and ill intentions, I don't want him. Plus, I think he's a little too cocky for me. My attitude is always on a thousand, so I doubt he's going to wanna put up with that."

"Can you stop being a baby all the time and take risks," Jolani chimed in, nudging my shoulder.

"I'm not being a baby. The only reason he's looking my way is because I helped him out with his history paper. His ass might want me to help him with another assignment in English," I scoffed.

"Girl, please. Look, you've been talking about wanting to be with him since freshman year. Go after that man."

"She doesn't have to go after him now. He's coming over here,"

Jolani let me know, nudging my shoulder.

I rolled my eyes, seeing how excited the females were, how they gawked over Kadarius like he was a prized possession. He approached me with a smile as bright as the sun. The sweat glistened off of his chocolate skin like diamonds.

"Wassup, bookworm?" he greeted.

"Wassup, jockstrap?"

"Oh, you got jokes." He laughed.

"I always do."

"So, you not gonna congratulate a nigga on the big win tonight?" He smiled with glee.

"Congratulations on winning the homecoming game."

"I've wanted to ask you something for a while now. You just always look busy, so I don't ask."

"I'm a busy woman."

"Well, I love a busy woman who stays on her shit."

"Hmm, I love a man who respects a busy woman's schedule."

"How about you quit playing and be my girl already?"

"Oh shit, big daddy done did it now," Angela's corny ass chimed in, covering her mouth, making all of us laugh.

"Be your girl, huh?"

"You heard me."

"I thought you had about three, four, or probably more of those."

"Where?"

"All over, you act like I don't know who you are."

"You tryna call me a hoe?"

"That's what it seems like. You don't stick to one girl."

"I'm trying to make you my one and only girl."

"Boy, please." I laughed.

"I can show you if you give me an answer."

"Fine, I'll give you one chance and one chance on. Now show me, Mr. Norwood."

"I will, Mrs. Norwood."

I was knocked from my flashback by Jolani calling my name. I didn't even know she walked in.

"The hell got you all spaced out?" she asked, coming over and pulling me into a hug.

"Nothing, just thinking. Wassup with you?"

"Girl nothing, I've wanted to tell you about something, but I haven't had the time."

"Tell me what?"

"A bitch is not single no more!" she squealed like a love-sick teen.

"Oh lord, I pray for the man," I joked.

"Girl shut up, he's amazing. I think he can be the one this time."

"This time out of the others. I hope so. You always jump into relationships quickly, Jojo," I replied, calling her by her nickname.

"I know, I'm serious this time, though."

"I hope so."

"Mama, I'm thirsty," Cassie voiced, coming from the side of the dryer.

"Hey, Jolani, can you go to the vending machine outside and get her something to drink?"

"Of course, come on, niecy." She smiled, grabbing Cassie's hand, and walking outside.

I looked down at my hands to see I still had Kadarius jersey in my hand. Suddenly, there was that wave of hurt attacking my heart again. I quickly wiped my tears away and threw the jersey in a nearby trash can.

"Tears don't look good on a beautiful woman."

I turned around and quickly wiped my eyes, seeing Raymon standing there with a look of concern on his face.

"I'm not even in the mood to argue with you right now. What are you doing here?" I sighed.

"To talk to you."

"How did you know I was here? Are you fucking following me? Raymon, I swear to God if I have to call the police, I will."

"I just want us to work. You don't understan—"

"No, you don't understand. I don't want you. There is no us."

"There was always an us. I know you miss the way I kissed you, the way I touched you. You can't blame being married as a reason for us not to be together, because as far as I can see your single now."

"How the hell do you know if I'm single or not?"

"That empty finger tells a lot. Just stop playing these games and be my woman. We can do what we did at the hotel like last time. I know you want it."

"You're fucking delusional."

Before I could go off, how I wanted, Cassie and Jolani came back in. When they bought their eyes to Raymon, Cassie ran to me and clung onto my leg for dear life, while Jolani pulled Raymon into a hug and kissed him on his lips.

"Good, you guys met one another. Celeste, this is my boyfriend Raymon, baby this is my best friend, Celeste."

"Celeste and I were just talking, and I was just telling her about you."

If looks could kill, Raymon would have been six feet under within milliseconds.

Chapter 25: It's Not Adding Up

Kadarius

"What you want to do today, man?"

"It doesn't matter. We can play some video games and watch movies."

"My man. I'll order pizza. What's wrong with your sister?"

"She said she's having a hard time with you and mom being apart, but I think it's more than that. I think there's something she isn't telling me. Well, I know there is. I can feel it."

"I'll have your mom talk to her. What about you, though? How do you feel about this situation?"

"It sucks. Did you move because of me? I know I've been giving you a hard time. I just missed being around you?"

Hearing my son ask me if he was the reason my wife and I weren't together broke my heart. When I did that shit with Reggie, it never dawned on me that the shit could blow up in my face. Now because of my actions, my kids were suffering. I explained to KJ that none of this was his fault. I told him daddy made a mistake and had to fix. I knew that last part was a lie. There was no way in hell Celeste would take me back. In her eyes, I had done the unforgivable. In mine, she just needed time to cool off.

KJ started playing the new *Grand Theft Auto* game I got him yesterday while I sat and thought about the events that had taken place the last couple of months. That night Celeste showed me that video, I felt like somebody had knocked the wind out of me. To make matters worse, we found cameras in the house. I racked my brain, trying to figure out who could have done it. I came to the conclusion that it was Reggie. I went to his firm the next day to confront him.

"You son of a bitch!" I yelled as I walked into his office and charged at him.

"What the hell is wrong with you, KD? This is my office! Calm your ass down."

"Don't tell me to calm down after the shit you pulled."

He played dumb like he didn't know what I was talking about.

"Don't play dumb, nigga. How dare you plant cameras in my house!"

"Cameras? How the hell would I plant cameras in your house? Why would I want to see you and your wife together?"

"To ruin my marriage. You planted that camera in my man cave, sucked me off, and then sent the video to my wife. Give me one good reason I shouldn't kill you."

I threw him against the wall, which caused his secretary to run in. She asked Reggie if he wanted her to call security. He knew better than to call the police on me, so he declined and made her leave us alone.

"KD, you gotta believe me, I didn't put cameras in your house. How would I get in? How would I get your wife's information to send it to her?"

"Just like you found her at the book event."

"Look, like I told you, I didn't do it. Look on the bright side though, at least we don't have to hide anymore."

Reggie was making me more pissed off than I already was. If he thought for one second that we would be together, he was wrong. I punched him in the face a few times and told him to stay the fuck away from my family and me."

"Dad? Dad?" KJ called.

"My bad, son, what's up?"

"I think the pizza man is at the door."

I got up and went to the door. The pizza was already paid for, so all I had to do was sign for it. Once I was finished at the door, I sat the pizza down on the table and told KJ to dig in. We started laughing and talking while we ate. It felt good to spend time with my son. Messing around with Reggie caused me to miss out on moments like this. Now that he was out of the picture, moments like this would happen more often. The only thing that was missing was Cassie being here. I decided to call her on FaceTime.

"What Kadarius?" Celeste answered with an attitude.

"Where's Cassie?"

"She's in her room. We were about to go to the spa, but she freaked out for some reason. She won't tell me what's wrong."

"Let me talk to her."

She went into Cassie's room and gave her the phone.

"What's wrong, baby girl?" I questioned.

"Daddy, I wanna come to your house."

"I thought you wanted to stay with your mom?" I asked, looking confused.

"I changed my mind. Will you come get me?"

I was about to tell her, yes, but Celeste told me she was headed out and would drop her off. KJ was excited when I told him Cassie was coming. They argued at times, but they hated being away from each other. At first, I wondered if that's what was wrong with Cassie, but pushed that idea out my head. The look in her eyes told me it was deeper than that. I wasn't sure what was wrong, but I was damn sure going to find out.

Chapter 26: Special Affair

Celeste

"Are you sure you don't wanna tell me what's going on?" I asked Cassie, looking over at her in the passenger's seat. She hugged onto her stuff bear, staring outside of the window, watching the rain glide down the glass.

"Cassie Bug, come on, you always tell me everything." I sighed.

Seeing that she didn't feel like talking, I left it alone. Pulling into Kadarius' yard. I beeped the horn a few times before he came outside with an umbrella. As soon as Cassie saw him, she jumped out of the car and ran into his arms. He picked her up, and she wrapped her arms around his neck, embracing him as tight as a spider monkey.

"Can you please talk to her and find out what's going on?"

"I will. Stay safe in this weather."

"Okay," I replied, cutting the conversation short.

After telling Cassie bye, I made my way to the closest bar in the area. I needed quality time to myself because I was still trying to cope with this divorce. I needed to get this weight off my chest, so I even called Jolani and Charlotte to have a few drinks with me.

I pulled up to the bar and killed the engine in my car, getting out, making my way inside. Since Jolani and Charlotte weren't there yet, I decided to order my drinks ahead of time. Grabbing a seat, I sighed and pulled my phone out, looking at my lock screen, which was a photo of Cassie and KJ as babies.

"What can I start you off with?" the bartender asked, placing a napkin in front of me.

"Can I get a Rémy Martin XO?"

"Of course," he replied, grabbing a bottle off the back shelf, and pouring some in a glass, putting it in front of me.

"Thanks."

I picked at my all-white stiletto nails, before twirling my finger around the rim of the glass. "Special Affair" by The Internet played throughout the building as I downed my drink, feeling the cognac burn the back of my throat like hot coals.

"Damn, you drinking without us?" Charlotte voiced with Jolani right beside her. I laughed lightly and shook my head before watching them take a seat next to me.

"I had to get an early start for the bullshit I'm about to tell you two."

"Oh Lord, please don't be pregnant," Charlotte joked.

"Oh God, no, it's about Kadarius."

"Still having trouble in paradise?"

"Paradise is underrated."

I laughed to myself, downing the rest of what was in the glass. I raised my empty glass, and the bartender hit me with another. Charlotte gave me a look of concern, not ever seeing me like this before.

"What's going on?" Jolani quizzed with worry drenched

in her voice.

"Kadarius and I are getting a divorce," I replied, letting the tears fall like the rain outside.

"I'm so sorry, Celly," Charlotte expressed, pulling me into a side hug.

"What happened?" Jolani asked.

"He's gay. He was fucking another man in my house."

"Damn, I'm sorry to hear that, Celly. When did you find out?"

"The day I was in Cali for the movie launch. It was the day he was supposed to pick the kids up from camp, and they caught a fucking cold waiting in the rain for him. The entire time he was getting his dick sucked by another man, he was supposed to be there for our fucking kids!" I yelled, tossing the drink back, feeling that numbing sensation take over. I slammed the glass on the table, quickly wiping my eyes with my sleeve.

"It will be okay," Jolani encouraged.

"No! It's not going to be okay, Jojo! I put everything on the line for that man, I put my life on hold once I got pregnant with the twins he wanted, I wasn't ready for kids, but he wanted a family, so I stopped everything for what he wanted! I didn't plan on having kids as soon as I got fresh out of college. I put starting my writing career on hold for his fucking football career that never happened, and I spent almost a million dollars getting him to where the hell he is now! I paid for the building he built his firm up in. He only put in six thousand on fucking thirty thousand dollar building I paid for! That house, I bought that shit, I built that nigga up, and he does me like this!" I yelled, feeling the pain tighten in my chest.

"You will be okay," Charlotte assured, rubbing my back to soothe me.

"No, the hell I'm not. It took everything in me not to hurt

him. If it weren't for our kids, I would have fuck Kadarius up! I could handle him cheating with a woman because that can be fixed. Charlotte, daddy cheated on mama, and they went to counseling and got better. I could see if he fucked around with a woman. Yeah, that's something we need to talk about like grown ass adults because mama and daddy told me that a marriage is far from perfect, but a man! A fucking man!" I cried.

"Look, he didn't deserve you because you're one hell of a woman. You've done things for him that a basic bottom of the bucket bitch would have never done. His ass would have had to work a corner to get that big ass nice building he's in. You worked your ass off, and I'm proud of that. You're an excellent mother and an amazing author. Any man would *kill* to be with you, fuck him." Charlotte spoke, getting angry herself. As a big sister, she didn't like to see me hurt, and seeing me hurt now made her blood boil.

"I can't do this. It hurts me so bad guys. If I were an evil bitch, I would file for full custody of the kids, but I'm not doing that because I know how much the kids love him. I've been through so much, and for me to start over is something that I can't do. I wasted years on this man!"

"Look, it will take some time, but you're a strong woman. You got this, baby sis."

∞ ∞ ∞

We drank and ate for a good two hours before I sent both women on their way. As bad as they wanted to drive me home because I was wasted, I decided against it. Jolani worked as an FBI agent, so she had to work early in the morning, and Charlotte had my niece to get back to since it was getting late.

"Another shot," I said, pushing my glass up to the bartender.

"Are you sure?" he asked, concerned with how drunk I was.

"No, she's not. She's fine." I turned around to see Raymon's goofy ass standing there with concern in his eyes. He took a seat next to me and sighed.

"What are you doing to yourself, Mrs. Norwood," he said, placing his hand on mine from reaching for the glass.

"I'm Ms. Braxton now."

"Celeste Braxton, huh?"

"You damn skippy, what do you want?"

"What's going on with you? I don't see that glow you had last time I saw you."

"Raymon, if you don't want me to bust you in your shit with this glass, I advise you get out of my space."

"I'm genuinely asking out of concern. What's wrong?"

It was as if what's wrong was the trigger for the tears to be pulled because I ended up crying again.

"Am I not pretty enough? Am I ugly? Am I too intelligent? Do I come over rude? Am I to fucking invasive? What's wrong with me?" I cried, looking down. Raymon grabbed me by the chin and lifted my face.

"There's nothing wrong with you. You're beautiful, smart, inquisitive, and your energy is bright. Stop asking what's wrong with you and start asking yourself what's not wrong with you. Your beautiful, Celeste."

"Make me feel beautiful again."

Raymon slid a hundred-dollar bill on the table and grabbed my hand, pulling me outside to his car, which was parked far. Once we got in his car, he grabbed my face and pressed his lips against mine.

"I'm gonna kiss away all the ugly part of you that you

think you have," he mumbled against my lips.

We stripped out of our clothes before I found myself riding him like a motorcycle in the backseat. He held onto my back and latched onto my hardened nipple. I ran my fingers through his waves, moaning in his ear.

"Tell me your mine," he demanded, smacking my ass, making me moan louder from the intense pleasure.

"I'm about to cum." I said, almost out of breath.

"Tell me your mine, and I'll let you cum," he said, grabbing my neck, tightening his grip on it, turning me on.

"Fuck, I'm yours!" I screamed, bouncing on his dick.

Raymon dug his nails into my waist, and I dug mine into his shoulder as he came inside me, and I came on him. I rested my head on his shoulder as he massaged my ass, still in the same position.

"You're always gonna be mine, don't forget that. I love you, Celeste."

Chapter 27: It Was Good Until It Wasn't

Raymon

I was in my home smoking a blunt, planning a vacation to Dubai for Celeste and me. After she said the words that I've wanted to hear from her since day one, five days ago, I've been on cloud nine. The entire time I've been yearning for another piece of her, and now that I finally had it with a hint of confirmation, I felt as if my plan was falling right into place.

After I booked the flight for next week, I pulled my phone out and went to my gallery. After the steamy car sex we had, she passed out in my car. I took it upon myself to collect some trophies, taking a few naked photos of her. I bit my lip, thinking about pounding her shit from the back while she was handcuffed. I came across the picture of her lying on her back with her legs open, and I even admired the small little beauty mark she had on her inner thigh.

When I heard a knock on my front door, I sighed, locking my phone, and walking downstairs. When I went downstairs, I looked out of my window to see it was Jolani. I sighed to myself, not wanting to let her in. If she didn't see my car in the front, I would have pretended not to be home. Part of me wanted to know how the hell she knew where I lived. I turned around to see that I had photos printed out of Celeste all over my kitchen table. *Shit,* I thought to myself, automatically coming to a panic. I rushed to the door and walked out instead of inviting her inside.

"What are you doing here?" I asked, looking down at her.

"You weren't answering my calls, Raymon. You've been ignoring me for five days, what's going on?" she quizzed with crossed arms.

"How did you know where I stay?"

"You left your wallet in my car last week, remember. I looked in your wallet and remembered seeing your address on your license. Now answer my question."

"I've been busy."

"Mhm, yeah, right. Raymon, I've been hurt way to many times to know when a nigga is tryna dog me out. Are you leading me on?"

"Look, Jello, I mean Jojo—"

"Are you serious right now?" she scoffed.

"I just woke up, and I'm tired okay. I told you I've been busy. I would never dog you out, baby." I sighed, pulling her into my arms.

"Really?"

"Yes, really," I replied, pecking her lips once before pecking her all over her face, making her laugh.

"Thank you."

"You don't have to thank me. I'm your man, girl. Stop acting like I'm up to no good."

"Fine, I just get a little self-conscious about myself and my relationship sometimes, babe. you just have to bear with me."

"I know."

"Good, so now that I'm calm, how about we have a little fun in the bedroom. I'll even let you do what you suggested last time."

Jolani smiled, tugging at my earlobe. I licked my lips and smiled, not wanting to turn down the offer. All the other women that I've been through, Jolani was the only one who could handle my dominant side in the bedroom, and I loved it.

"I'm down for that."

"Great, let's go." She smiled, trying to reach for my doorknob, but I stopped her.

"How about we do it at your place."

"No babe, I'm horny right now. I can't wait until we get to my place. While we're at it, you can give me a little tour of your house." She smiled.

Hesitant, I chewed on my bottom lip, then sighed.

"How about this? Go sit in your car and I'll get you after I finish straightening up some stuff. I don't like to have people in my house when it's not up to par."

"Babe, I don't mind a junky house." She smiled.

"Well, I don't like inviting people in my home while it's not at its best."

"Okay, I respect that. Come get me out the car when you're ready," she replied, pecking my cheek, and going to her car.

I walked inside and rushed to my kitchen table, grabbing all the photos, trying to figure out where to stash them. I decided to throw them in the trash bin for now. Once I looked around to see that everything else was good, I called Jolani inside. She smiled and looked around my house in awe.

"This is neat. You sure know how to decorate."

"Thanks, I try."

"You can say that again."

"Want anything to drink?" I asked, walking over to the fridge.

"No, I think I like it better if I give you something to

drink," she replied, strutting over to me.

"Oh, I like that too." I smirked, pulling her into my arms.

As soon as I was about to get busy, my phone started ringing. I sighed and pulled it out my pocket, and as soon as I saw the caller I.D, happiness drowned my body like a wave.

"Give me a minute," I replied, walking off to another room.

"Sure."

I answered the phone, smiling just hearing Celeste's voice on the other end.

"We need to talk," she said.

"You're right about that. I've been meaning to talk to you too."

"About what happened it wa—"

"It was amazing. I forgot how good it felt to be insi—"

"It wasn't supposed to happen. Raymon, I was drunk and emotional. What happened was a mistake."

"You and these fucking mistakes." I laughed angrily to myself.

"Because it was a mistake, I was confused, hurt, and drunk. Raymon, I was vulnerable, and what we did was crossing the line. I'm sorry for pursuing you. That was my fault. Raymon, I need you to stay away from me."

I chuckled to myself, feeling that flip switch yet again. Did Celeste think she would lead me on and expect that I would leave her alone?

"I've been trying to pursue you for a minute now. I'm not a man who takes the answer no pretty well. You said it yourself, your mine. You can call the cops, get a restraining order, do what you have to do, but I'm not gonna back down from getting what I want, and you Celeste Braxton, is what I want."

"Are you crazy or are you delusional, Raymon, I'm only gonna say this once, stay the hell away from me and stay away from my best friend."

"I don't give a fuck what you say, princess. Just know, I'm gonna go through anybody to get to you, including your best friend, and if I have to, taking out your faggot ass soon to be ex-husband is light work to me. I have a little trip for us to take next week, if you don't meet me at my place next week Friday at noon, you're gonna see a side of me you've never seen before. You remember where I live, so you've got an hour to meet me at my place, or somebody's gonna get hurt." I didn't even give Celeste a chance to say anything before I hung up.

"Raymon, what's this?" asked Jolani walking toward me with the photos of Celeste.

Chapter 28: Dangerous Secrets

Jolani Harris

We hurt people that love us, love people that hurt us
~Kendrick Lamar

Being an FBI agent has taught me a sense of awareness when it comes to people. Whenever a man pursued me heavily, I did a full background check on him. I needed to know if he had a criminal record if his family members were crazy if he had a football team of kids with dumb bitches, and if he had a good job. Normally, I would run a guy's background before going too far, but Raymon was so charming that I decided to let my guard down a little. That was a big mistake.

When I ran his name, nothing came up. I mean absolutely nothing. To most, that would be a good thing, but to me, it was a red flag. In my world, a clean background meant a person wasn't who they said they were. I uploaded a picture of Raymon that I had taken to a facial recognition software I had and still came up with nothing, which was another red flag. Something definitely wasn't right.

I had had this man around my best friend and goddaughter, so I needed to find out what he was hiding. I went to his house, pretending to be horny in hopes that he would leave me alone in his room at some point so that I can snoop. When Raymon told me that he had to make a call, I took that to my advantage. The first thing I did was look in the trash. What I found shocked me. There were several pictures of Celeste. Some of her at different book events, dropping the kids off at my house, and even in her yard.

"Raymon, what's this?"

"It's not what you think it is."

"Not what I think? It looks like you're stalking my best friend."

"Stalking is such a horrible word. I prefer to call it admiring."

"Admiring? You got issues. I'm getting the hell out of here. Stay away from Celeste and me!"

I ran out the door before he could say another word. I heard Raymon calling my name, but I didn't turn around. I sped to my house, went inside, and tried to call Celeste. For whatever reason, her phone was going straight to voicemail. I left her a message telling her to call me back as soon as she got the message.

Bang...bang...bang!

"Jolani, open the door!"

"Raymon, go away before I call the police!" I yelled.

"Just let me explain."

"I don't need you explaining shit to me. Get the fuck away from my door."

He continued to bang on my door. I heard him talking about how he pursued me to get closer to Celeste. He mentioned them having sex and her cutting him off. Realizing he was crazier than I thought, I ran to my room to get my gun out of my Chester drawer. I heard what sounded like glass breaking. I made sure my gun was loaded and went to see what was going on.

"Raymon, get the hell out of my house!" I screamed when I saw him pacing around my living room.

"You didn't let me explain!"

"I heard what you said through the door, and I don't need to hear anything else. Now get the hell out of my house and stay the fuck away from me and my best friend!" I yelled, pointing my gun at him.

I thought the gun would scare him away, but it didn't. Instead, he came charging at me. We started tussling and wrestling over the weapon. He was trying to get it away from me while I was trying to hold on to it so I could shoot.

Pow!

The gun went off. I looked at Raymon to see where I had shot him, but he didn't have any blood on him. Suddenly, I felt like I was losing consciousness. That's when I realized I had been shot in the chest. I dropped to the floor. Not wanting to die, I started trying to crawl to my phone, but Raymon stopped me.

"This didn't have to happen, you know. All you had to do was play your role. Now I will have to help Celeste grieve over you."

"Help," I whispered.

"Help? You want help after the trouble you've caused? I don't think so. In fact, I will leave you right here. Maybe in your next life, you will learn to mind your business."

He got up and walked away from me. When I heard the door close, I started trying to crawl again, but it was no use. In the midst of trying to get to my phone, I faded out. This wasn't how I thought my life would end. I prayed to God that my best friend didn't suffer the same fate as me.

Chapter 29: Let Me Be Your Man

Celeste

I can't live my life without you (oh, baby)
Every time I see you walkin' by, I get a thrill
You don't understand, but in time you will
I must make you understand
~Zapp & Roger

I sighed, racking my nerves trying to get Jolani to answer my calls. I needed to warn her about Raymon, especially after the conversation we had over the phone.

"Shit!" I yelled, seeing that she sent me to voicemail for the tenth time. I felt as if I let things get too far out of hand, and everything was coming back to bite me in my ass. After putting pieces together, it hit me that Raymon placed those cameras in my home, and that's how he e-mailed me that video. How could I be so oblivious to his trickery? Was I so stuck up in my ways to not look more into this man? Part of me felt like a whore for fucking around with a man I didn't know from a can of paint.

How could I let him touch me, let alone persuade me? It was as if he was playing this mind game with me, and I was losing endlessly. It was as if it wasn't one thing it was another. I was still trying to cope with this Kadarius situation, my career on my shoulders, and Raymon turning into this huge creep. Sadly, part of me blamed myself for losing control while drunk. I knew after he dropped me home that night, and I woke up with regret. I had to kill the situation before it grew. When the conversation didn't go as planned, I stood by my word on calling the police.

I found the nearest parking spot and got out of my car, heading inside of the police station. After approaching the front desk and asking for a detective, I took a seat in the waiting area. Within minutes, a detective finally called me in his office. Once I took a seat in front of him, he gave me his undivided attention.

"What can I do for you, Mrs. Norwood?" he asked.

"I have a problem I feel as if I need to report before it gets worse."

"What problem is that?"

"I think I have a stalker on my hands."

"I'm sorry to hear that. Tell me what's been going on," he replied, taking out a notepad and a pen.

"Okay, uh, a few months back, I met this guy. His name is Raymon, Raymon Stevens. He said he was one of my fans, and I even attended a few meetings he had planned for his book club. However, it seems as if everywhere I turn, he pops up, I even told him to stop following me, and he continued. He even went deeper into messing around with my best friend to get closer to me. I called him today to tell him to stop before I get the cops involved, and I guess that didn't faze him."

"Mhmm, may I ask you a few questions, Mrs. Norwood?"

"Of course?"

"Have you had any sexual interactions with Mr. Stevens?" he asked, catching me off guard. I knew for a fact that question would come because I tried to leave the explicit details out of it the best I could.

"Excuse me?"

"Have you and Mr. Stevens been sexually interacting?"

"Why does it matter? Why are you asking me this?"

"Mrs. Norwood, we're not going to get anywhere unless you tell me the truth."

"Okay, yes, we have, but what does it have to do with him stalking me?"

"It has a lot to do with it. Mr. Steven came into my office last week and told me you were stalking him."

"What?" I yelled in disbelief.

"Mrs. Norw—"

"No, he's stalking me! He's fucking crazy!"

"Calm down, can you do that? Look, he said you've been e-mailing him and contacting him left and right. He said that you sent him sexual texts and even sent him threats."

"Where's the proof?"

"I have e-mails and messages."

"Show me."

He opened his laptop before logging in and clicking away before turning the screen to me. My jaw dropped in confusion, seeing my actual e-mail address at the top of the screen. I placed my hand over my mouth seeing a photo of me naked. It was the same photo I sent Kadarius. We were married, so I sent my husband photos of me, and he returned the gesture. The thing was, how was it sent to Raymon? What the hell was I looking at?

"Where's your proof, Mrs. Norwood?" he countered, closing his laptop while I was still looking.

"That's not me! I swear to God that isn't me sending him pictures and messages!"

"I advise you to leave before you dig yourself into a whole heap of trouble, Mrs. Norwood."

"But I ha—"

"I hope what you're about to say is that you have more proof than expired text messages."

I opened my mouth to try and say something, but I decided against it. I grabbed my purse and stormed out to my car.

Getting inside, I punched the steering wheel.

"Fuck!" I yelled, throwing my phone into the passenger seat.

Since this was getting me nowhere, I decided to visit Jolani personally to see if she could listen to me and help me out with this situation. It wasn't like her not my answer my calls, so I knew for a fact that something was wrong, I had to go see her.

It didn't take me long before I arrived at Jolani's place. Killing the engine in my car, I got out and approached the house slowly. When I noticed the window was broken, my heart shattered in my chest, scared that I was thinking the worst. I grabbed her spare key from the flowerpot and opened the door.

"Jojo! Are you here?" I called out, looking around each corner, receiving no answer.

"Jolani! Answer me, sis. I've been calling you for hours! Where are you?" I yelled, walking all over the house. When I turned the corner, I slid into something and almost busting my ass on the floor.

"Shit!" I yelled, holding my side.

When I looked down, I noticed that blood covered my hands and pants. I started shaking, and my eyes watered, seeing Jolani only a few inches away from me lying on the floor, pale and lifeless. Her luscious smooth skin was now flushed, and her eyes were cold, looking up at the ceiling. I screamed with tears cascading down my face like a river, I knew that I wasn't supposed to touch her body, but I pulled her dead body in my arms anyway, brushing her hair from her face.

"Come on, no, you can't be gone, Jojo, no!" I sobbed, rocking her body in my arms. I knew she was gone not only because of the hole in her chest, but her body was dead weight, and it was cold.

I dug in my pocket and pulled out my phone. I grew frustrated from my fingers slipping across the screen due to the blood on my hands.

"Siri, call 911." I sniffled, still holding Jolani.

After calling the police, I sat my phone to the side, still taking in the death of my best friend, my sister. As soon as the police arrived, they took Jolani's body and I gave my statement. I sat on the porch with tears in my eyes, watching them zip the black bag over her face — the face that I was going to have sawed in my brain for the rest of my life.

When I saw Kadarius pull up and get out of his car, he ran over to me and pulled me into his arms.

"She's gone. She's really gone," I cried into his chest.

"I know." He sighed, rubbing my back to comfort me.

"She was my sister, Kadarius! She was my best friend!" I cried louder, feeling that tightening sensation in my chest.

"I know everything will be okay."

"No, it's not! She's dead. He killed her!" I cried, thinking of how Raymon could have possibly taken my best friend's life.

"Who?"

"The guy from the club, Raymon. He killed her."

"How do you know?"

"Because he's been fucking stalking me! He's been trying to get in my fucking head, Kadarius! He's fucking crazy!"

"You gonna take me to this nigga place, and I'm gonna show him who he fucking with," he said, getting hyped.

"No! You can't afford to get in trouble, Kadarius."

"Did you at least go to the police?"

"Yes? I think he hacked me or something, but he made it seem as if I was the crazy one like I was the one stalking him. The police aren't going to do anything."

"Look, we can get this settled more tomorrow. Let's get

you out of these bloody clothes and relaxed, okay."

I nodded my head as he walked me over to my car. I got in the driver seat and ran my hands through my hair.

"You need me to follow you home?" he asked, leaning on my car.

"No, I'm fine. Just get to my kids. If he could do something like this, I'm afraid he'll go further. I'll stop by tomorrow to see them. I just need time to clear my head right now."

"Okay, call me when you get home."

"I will," I replied, watching him walk back over to his car.

I pulled out of the yard and made my way home, trying to keep the tears from flowing. Jolani wouldn't intentionally hurt anybody, and for someone to hurt her deliberately didn't sit right with me. For that someone to possibly be Raymon wasn't sitting right with me.

I pulled up to my home and killed the engine in my car, getting out. Unlocking my front door, I closed it and ran upstairs to get out of these bloody clothes. The feeling of it sticking to my skin was getting to me, and it was already bad enough that being in this big house alone with the picture of my best friend's dead face stuck in my head was killing me.

Stripping out of my clothes, I jumped into my shower. I watched as the blood collided with the water as it went down the drain. Running my hands down my face, I sighed, finally deciding to go stay with Charlotte tonight. My mind wouldn't let me stay here alone. As soon as I got out of the shower, my heart almost jumped out of my chest upon hearing "I Wanna Be Your Man" by Zapp and Rogers playing off my Alexa home system.

"Kadarius?" I called out. Throwing my robe over my shoulders. As soon as I opened the door, I screamed when all the lights turned off.

"Alexa, turn on the lights," I commanded. "Alexa, turn on

the lights!" I said louder, seeing that she wasn't turning on the lights.

I grew paranoid, so I grabbed one of my razors, easing out of the bathroom, trying to look around the semi-pitch-black bedroom. As soon as I stepped all the way out of the bathroom, I swallowed the lump in my throat, seeing someone sit at the end of my bed looking down.

"This is a classic. You can never go wrong with Zapp and Roger."

"Raymon, get out of my house."

"You ever been to Paris?"

"I'm not going to ask you again," I said, preparing to cut his ass with this razor.

"Why do you still treat me like this, Celeste?" Raymon quizzed, getting up and making me step back.

"Get the hell out of my house!" I yelled.

"You don't remember me, huh?"

I gripped the razor in my hand, seeing that he had my cell phone in his hands as well. As soon as I tried to run, he grabbed me. With a quick reflex, I slashed his face with the razor making him stumble back. As soon as he fell on the floor holding his face, I ran out of the room, screaming for help, hoping one of my neighbors would hear me.

As soon as I tried to head down the stairs, I felt a tugging at my hair, and I was pushed into the wall. When I tried to cut Raymon again, he grabbed my arm, making me drop the razor and pinned it behind my back. The next thing I knew, he slammed my head into the wall knocking me out cold.

Chapter 30: Hurt People

Kadarius

That ain't even my intention, baby
You know that you're all that I've got
And I never meant to hurt us, baby
I'm just tryna learn how to love
~Sabrina Claudio

After leaving Celeste, I found myself back at my apartment with the kids. While they were watching TV, I was in my room on my laptop looking up information on this Raymon dude. It was off that I was researching for hours and couldn't find any type of information on this man. I couldn't even get his birthday to pull up. My cop friends couldn't even give me anything on him. When I didn't get a call back from Celeste, I picked my phone up from the nightstand and dialed her number. When it went to voicemail automatically, so I tried again just to be sent to voicemail once again.

I assumed that she didn't want to be bothered since she just lost Jolani, but I was still worried about her. Celeste was the type of person to grieve in silence, and that worried me about her the most. As soon as I was about to call her again, I saw my assistant's name pop up on the screen. Sighing, I answered and heard the worry in her voice.

"Mr. Norwood, I'm sorry to reach out to you so late, but there's been an issue."

"What type of issue, Janet?"

"Check your e-mail."

"What? You need to check it now."

"Okay, I'm at my laptop right now."

I opened my e-mail account and saw that there was an e-mail sent out to me along with everyone with everybody else in my firm, even the cleaning staff. I clicked the e-mail, and my eyes grew wide, seeing a collage of photos of Reggie and me in bed. In all of these photos, I was passed out while Reggie was lying on my chest, posing. I felt my blood boiling, there was even a photo of me completely naked and the caption was *Mr. and Mr. Norwood, my husband and I are with you LGBTQ community.*

I knew exactly who did this, and it pointed me in Reggie's direction. I knew he was upset with me for throwing him to the side, and I knew for a fact he was upset with me for not being there for a gay client who was framed for killing a married man. I didn't want to seem homophobic, but I couldn't work with gay clients. I've been going by that memo since day one. It was weird going by it today now because I didn't wanna identify myself as being gay. I wasn't fucking gay. I classified myself as curious, and now that I knew for a fact on what I wanted, me being gay was out of the options.

"I'm gonna call you back, Janet," I replied, tossing my laptop to the side, and hanging up on her. I called Reggie, and he answered on the second ring.

"Did you get my e-mail?" He said. I could tell he was smirking through the phone.

"I'm gonna fucking kill you," I said through gritted teeth.

"It seems as if the only way you would hear me is if I got loud, now everybody knows about us. You should have taken on my offer a long time ago, KD."

"Do you think you gonna get away with this shit?" I said, pacing back and forth.

"I already have. All you had to do was let us be together."

"We were never going to fucking be together, I love my wife, and I don't give a fuck how long it takes, I'm gonna get her back."

"That's funny. I thought you knew me well enough to know that I don't give up easily."

"You won't be getting away with shit once I see you."

"I already have. See you soon, Mr. Norwood," Reggie remarked, hanging up on me.

I threw my phone on my bed, and frantically paced the floor. This shit was sent to all my colleagues and even people above me. I knew people would be on my ass as soon as I step foot into my firm next week. I felt as if I were about to pass the fuck out.

"Shit, Shit, shit," I mumbled, trying to calm down.

"Daddy, KJ fell asleep on me," Cassie voiced, coming into my bedroom with her covers over her shoulders.

"He did?" I asked, turning to her calming down.

"Yeah, can I sleep in here with you?"

"Yeah, princess, come on."

I got in bed with her, and she snuggled up to me. Just having her close to me made me have the sense of calmness I was trying to find not long ago. Cassie was slowly coming back to her old self, and after pushing her continuously to find out what was wrong with her, she was persistent with telling me nothing was wrong. I knew for a fact that her behavior would go straight out the window as soon as Celeste and I tell her about Jolani.

I reached over and grabbed my laptop, closing all the tabs, as soon as I was about to close Raymon's photo, Cassie closed the laptop and pulled the covers over her head.

"What's wrong with you, Cassie?" I asked, raising an eyebrow at her.

"He's scary," she declared, sounding like she was about to cry.

"Who is?"

"The man on the laptop. That's Auntie Jojo's boyfriend."

"How do you know him?"

"He was at her house. I don't like him."

"Why?"

"He touched me here," she cried, pointing to her butt.

I felt my blood pressure rising, thinking of a grown ass man touching my six-year-old daughter. I pulled her into my arms, caressing her hair, paining me to see her cry.

∞∞∞

After she fell asleep in my arms, I tried to call Celeste back to talk about this Raymon nigga. I was on a mission to put his ass six feet under for fucking with my wife and touching my child. I grew aggravated getting sent to voicemail for what seemed like the thousandth time.

"Shit!" I ranted, trying to figure out my next move.

I called Charlotte over to watch the kids, and I found myself in my firm with my guru Justin.

"Still nothing on this bastard?" I asked, stroking my beard.

"It's loading. Give it a minute to check the database."

"I don't have a fucking minute, Justin!" I yelled, pacing the floor like a junkie.

"Well, you gotta wait."

"I know."

"While we're waiting, can we talk about that e-mail?" Justin asked.

"No."

"There's nothing wrong with being gay, Mr. Norwood."

"I'm not fucking gay!" I yelled in his face, making him jump.

"I'm just stating my opinion, sir."

"You don't get paid to state your fucking opinion, Justin."

"You're right. I'll shut up."

As soon as we heard a ping, we both looked at the laptop and information popped up from every direction.

"Sweet baby fucking Jesus," Justin voiced, taking off his glasses.

"What?"

"You said his name was Raymon Stevens, right?"

"Yeah?"

"Well, your Raymon Stevens is actually Tykell Banker."

"Tykell Banker? That sounds familiar."

"It should be. He attended the same college as you and graduated the same year too. Tykell Banker, he's a Gemini and has his bachelor's in computer science and an associate degree in business. He was the leader of the chess club, a member of the book club—"

"I don't give a fuck about what clubs he was in. Tell me who the fuck I'm dealing with?"

"Tykell Banker, oh shit. He was a mental patient in Atlanta, he has multiple personality disorder, and he's bipolar. He broke out of the hospital a while back, killing three nurses and injuring eight of them. Damn, this dude needs some help ASAP. It says he has multiple sexual assault charges against him. This dude is a whole rapist and a pedophile. He was even a suspect two years ago on this big case that was going on for a while."

"What case?"

"They found over thirty women buried in his yard back in Vegas, and all women were sexually assaulted and dismembered."

"This shit is sick," I responded, shaking my head in disgust at the articles.

"It gets sicker. You said he was after your wife, right?"

"Yeah."

"What's your wife's maiden name?"

"Celeste Baxter."

"He's been following your wife since college."

"What? How you know?"

"They have photos of every room in his house, and there's a whole shrine of your wife found in his closet. He has posters of her in her cheerleading gear freshman year, graduation photos, homecoming photos, even photos after graduation when she was working at McDonald's."

"Oh my god, I gotta get to my wife," I said in a panic, reaching for my keys.

I got on the elevator and made my way to Celeste's house.

Once there, I didn't even bother parking straight. I pulled my gun from my armrest and got out running up the steps. I noticed the door was cracked open. Pushing it open further, I called out her name and noticed the entire house was pitch dark. "I Wanna Be Your Man" by Zapp and Rogers echoed throughout the house. I jogged upstairs and stopped in my tracks, seeing blood on the wall.

Chapter 31: Forget Me Not

'Cause I'm just a soul whose intentions are good
Oh Lord, please don't let me be misunderstood
Don't let me be misunderstood
~Nina Simone

"Get me the hell out of here!" I screamed at the top of my lungs, hoping someone could hear me. I woke up not too long ago, chained to a bed in a log cabin. I felt the more I screamed and yelled, my voice was becoming sore.

"You always were the vocal type," Raymon spoke, coming into the room with breakfast on a tray.

"Raymon, if you don't let me go I'l—"

"You'll what? You're not gonna do a got damn thing, so you can shut the fuck up and make things easier on your end, or I'm gonna have to be a lot less subtle because you don't know how to keep your attitude to a fucking minimum. We can do shit the easy way or the hard way. It's your choice." he said, flashing me his knife to put fear in me. And he did just that, the last thing I needed for him to kill me because of me being reckless with my mouth. The thought of my kids automatically went through my mind, how I didn't want them to have to go through life without their mother.

"Answer me!" he yelled, making me jump.

"The easy way," I replied, trying my best not to let him see me cry.

"Good, open your mouth," Raymon ordered, taking a fork full of eggs, and placing them to my lips.

I shook my head no, and he grabbed my face roughly, squeezing my cheeks, making me open my mouth, and he shoved the food in. He placed his hand over my mouth to keep me from spitting it out. Closing my eyes, I let the tears roll down my cheek freely before chewing and swallowing. He removed his hands from my mouth before caressing my cheek.

"What do you want from me?" I sniffled.

"The same shit I wanted from you back in college, Celeste!" I yelled, tossing the tray of food to the floor, making me jump.

"What?" I asked, genuinely confused on what the hell he was talking about. I didn't even know we attended the same college. I was oblivious to who this man really was.

"You still don't remember me, huh?" He laughed to himself, pacing back and forth.

"No, I don't know who the hell you are."

"That's funny, I've been your biggest supporter since day one! Celeste Baxter, I know you fucking remember me! You know who the hell I am!" Raymon yelled in my face.

"I swear, I don't remember you." I cried, trying to avoid eye contact.

"That's funny because I remember you, I remember everything about you, Celeste. Mrs. Homecoming Queen, cheerleading captain, head of your very own book club. You were hot shit back in NCAT. Let's see if this rings a few bells. The short lil pipsqueak who pushed you to start the book club. I was the nigga who took you to lunch after every book club meeting to discuss your dreams and goals. And then you got with Mr. Quarterback and forgot about me. You let him put me down like I was nothing. You gave me false hope that we would be together since the day we met."

"I—"

"I know this is gonna hit the nail hard. I'm the one who pushed you to get your first book published. You told me I was your inspiration for your very first published novel, *Entangled Intelligence*."

"Tykell?" I asked with a raised eyebrow.

There was no way this could be who I thought it was. Tykell was short and skinny with glasses, and his voice was high pitched. The Tykell I knew had braces and wore button-up shirts every day. I haven't seen Tykell since he was sent off to a mental institution for killing our professor because he thought she wanted a relationship with him.

"In the flesh, baby." He smiled.

"You gotta be fucking kidding me," I scoffed.

"Nah, I'm not. That's all I wanted for you was to remember me, to give me attention, and to fucking look at me the way you looked at Kadarius' bitch ass."

"Tykell, let me go."

"I'm not doing that, because if I let you go, I will never get a chance to get you again."

"What? You never fucking had me the first time, Ty! Get me out of here."

"We all know what happens if I let you walk out of here. You will call the police, and you will go back to your fucking husband."

"Your damn right I'm calling the fucking police. You have me pinned up in a bed in nothing but my robe, you damn near bust my head open, you stalked me, and you killed my best friend. I know you did."

"You were always stuck in the past, see me, I'd like us to push for the future the same way I pushed you to have the future you're living now."

"So, what now? You're gonna hold me hostage here forever?"

"I will hold you hostage here until you realize that I'm right for you. I forgave you for everything you've done to me, so now it's time for reconciliation."

"I didn't do anything but be nice to you."

"Bullshit! You let me rot in that fucking mental institute and only visited me once! Once Celly, only fucking one! You told me that you were going to come back for me, and you never did. You told me that you would never forget me!" Ty yelled in my face.

I swallowed the lump in my throat, seeing the vein twitch on the side of his forehead. He was livid, and I could tell.

"You're not going to get away with this."

"I already have," he replied, walking out the door and slamming it.

I looked up at the chains that were restraining me, trying to figure out how the hell I would get out of here.

"Fuck!" I yelled, yanking at the chains.

∞∞∞

I just sat there, looking out the windows at the trees. Sitting here thinking finally gave me an idea. Tykell pictured this fantasy in his head with the both of us, and I decided on using that to my advantage to get the hell out of here.

Ty came back in with a book and a chair in his hands. He sat the chair beside me and took a seat, opening one of my books.

"You were in drama class, too, right?" he asked, tracing his hands down my leg.

"Yes."

"It's time for a little acting."

"What?"

"Morgan wasn't into BDSM, but her husband was working nonstop, and she hasn't seen him home in a while. She knew he always wanted to try BDSM to spice up their sex life, so she surprised him with just that. Morgan let Charlie tie her up to their California king bed, and she could see that fire in his eyes that he had a worldwide list of things he wanted to try on her. This is my favorite part," Ty replied, closing the book.

Ty then stood up and pulled his shirt over his head and climbed on top of me. I tried to calm my nerves, but I wreaked of fear. He pulled my robe open, revealing my bare skin, running his hands down my body, making my skin crawl. His hands brushed against my breasts before trailing down to my lower body. Tykell stopped in his tracks before getting up and playing "I Wanna be Your Man" on his phone.

"Remember this song?" He smiled, climbing back on top of me.

"Wait!" I yelled before he could go any further.

"Morgan liked BDSM after trying it the first time with Charlie. You always take control, Ty, I wanna take control," I spoke, hoping he would unchain me.

"Do I look stupid?"

"Ty, I want you, I want to get on top of you and take control. I wanna show you how sorry I am for putting you through what I put you through."

"Oh, do you?"

"I do," I replied, hoping he would let me out. My body was getting sore from being in the same position for hours.

He got off of me before walking out of the room and coming back seconds later with a key in his hands. He unlocked the chains from around my arms and legs and pulled me up roughly by my arms. I was planning to dart toward the door now that I was free, but as soon as I saw the gun in his hands, I swallowed the lump in my throat and approached him seductively. I pushed him down on the bed and planted kisses all over his tattoos on his chest. He massaged my ass while I ran my hands up and down his dick, which was on hard. He closed his eyes and moaned, digging his nails into my thigh.

When Tykell placed the gun on the headboard next to him, I grabbed his face and roughly kissed him. As soon as he saw me reaching for the gun, we wrestled one another to keep the other from grabbing it. I bit him and scurried away from his grasp, ignoring his screams of pain. I quickly grabbed the gun and ran out.

As soon as I looked at the front door, I noticed it was locked and required a combination and a key. I didn't even have time to look for another exit before Tykell caught me, pulling me back by my hair. I fired the gun and dropped it, and missed him, cursing to myself. He tried to rush to it, but I jumped on his back, punching him in his head. He slung me to the side, making me fall into a glass ottoman. I arched my back in pain, as shards of glass sliced my skin.

"You're one hard-headed ass bitch," he said, tucking his gun in the back of his pants, standing over me.

Tykell didn't even bother to make sure I was out of the glass before grabbing me. He dragged me through the glass, ignoring my agonizing screams. As soon as he had me in his arms, I pulled out a shard of glass, stabbing him in his neck, making him drop me and scream in pain.

"Fuck!" he yelled, trying to get the glass from his neck.

I quickly got up and watched him stumble back and forth, trying to regain consciousness. I grabbed another piece of glass from the floor and charged at him, stabbing him multiple times. Ty grabbed my hand, making me drop the glass, and the next thing I knew, he had his hands around my neck. I clawed at his hands, trying to gasp for air, but received no luck.

"If I can't have you, he won't either!" Tykell spat through gritted teeth, tightening his grip.

My vision grew blurry, and tears streamed my face. I didn't wanna die, and even after stabbing his ass multiple times, he had the strength of one hundred men. Noticing the glass still in his neck, I pushed it in further, making him let me go. Ty dropped to his knees and pulled the glass from his neck, coughing and spitting up blood. I grabbed a glass vase sitting off to the side and bashed him in his head with it, knocking him out clean. I took his gun and searched his pockets for a phone, calling the police.

After telling them what happened, I stood there over Tykell's body, scared that he would get up and kill me. I jumped out of fear, hearing him groan. Once he looked up at me and saw me pointing the gun at me, he laughed to himself.

"You think you got the upper hand, huh?" He laughed, holding his bleeding neck.

"Bitch, I have the gun. I know I have the upper hand."

"I had the upper hand since day one, sweetheart."

"What the hell are you talking about?"

"You think calling the cops and getting me locked up is gonna keep me away from you, Celeste."

"Your ass is going under the jailhouse, so I'm highly confident that it will. You will never see me again, and I'm certain about that."

"You're right. I might have to up my game when I get out of jail."

"Who said you're ever gonna get out?"

"I'm labeled as crazy. You don't know how many cases I've beat."

"You won't beat this one."

"Oh, I will, and when I do, I might just come after your daughter, sweet lil Cassie. She looks just like you, and she even smells like you."

"If you come near my daughter, I swear to God—"

"If I come near her *again* you mean. Cassie and I have already met personally. Hopefully, when she grows up, she gets a body like yours. Lord knows her ass is just as soft as yours."

I sent two bullets flying through Tykell's body before climbing on top of him, pistol-whipping him with the gun. I found myself crying, looking at his unconscious body. For him to talk about my child like that triggered me. Just thinking of him touching my child drove me insane.

I heard sirens getting closer. Closing my robe, I limped to the nearest window and climbed out, meeting the officers at the head of the road. They stopped and placed me in the car, rushing inside the house. While they were inside the house, another officer took my statement and gave me a blanket.

"Ma'am, you said you knocked your offender unconscious, right?"

"Yes."

"Don't be alarmed, but he's no longer in the house. We have officers searching the woods for hi-."

"What? No! I swear to God he was in there, I shot him twice, I stabbed him, he has to be dead!" I yelled, feeling myself starting to panic.

The female officer tried to calm me down, but I began to hyperventilate, and within seconds, I passed out just thinking about what Tykell would do next.

Chapter 32: Plan B

*Without an understanding of bad...how can
one truly have an appreciation of good
~Kevin Gates*

"Fuck!" I yelled as I ran through the woods trying to make my escape.

When I planned to take Celeste, I never thought it would go wrong. In my mind, she would give in to my advances, and we would be happily ever after. Instead, she not only realized my true identity, but she also shot and stabbed me. Luckily for me, I always had a backup plan. After running through the woods, I reached the backup car that I had waiting for me.

Once I got to the car, I drove back to my place in the city. Thankfully, Celeste had never been to this home. Therefore, I didn't have to worry about the police showing up here. I called this nurse chick I knew and told her I needed her help ASAP. Though I never used her, I paid her fifteen hundred dollars every month. She always asked why I paid her but never called her for anything. That's cause a nigga like me was always two steps ahead.

"Raymon, what the hell happened?" she asked when she saw me.

"No questions, remember?" I reminded her.

"Well, it looks like the bullets went straight through. I can't tell if they did any damage or not. The stab wounds aren't that deep, so I can stitch you up. I will start an IV to give you some antibiotics to prevent infection and some fluids. I can also numb you while I do the stitching."

"I don't care. Just do what you have to do to get me back going."

"You're going to need you to stay put for a couple of days."

That was perfectly fine for me. I knew the police would be looking for me everywhere. They wouldn't find me, though. Nothing I owned here was in my name. The only person who knew who I really was is Celeste, and as far as everybody knew, I was locked away in a mental institution. I had that part covered too in case they went looking. There was a guy I knew in high school who everyone said looked like my twin brother. Well, I paid my "twin brother" good money to play me. Even though I thought it would never come to this, I always made sure my tracks were covered.

While the nurse was stitching me up, I thought about what my next move would be. Trying to get Celeste again would be damn near impossible. I didn't have Jojo to use anymore. Killing her wasn't part of the plan, but she was starting to learn too much. Fucking a chick who worked for the FBI wasn't a good idea from the beginning. However, I did what I had to go to get close to Celeste.

For some reason, while I was thinking, Celeste's daughter popped in my head. That's when it hit me. If I couldn't get Celeste, her daughter would be the next best thing. Taking her would surely get a rise out of Celeste and make her come to me. Shortly after I formulated my plan in my head, I drifted off to sleep.

Two Days Later

Although I promised my nurse that I would stay put for a couple of days, I had been out watching Cassie, trying to decide when would be the best time to grab her. She was always with her brother and that bitch ass father of hers. They went to a local camp every day from eight in the morning to about five in the afternoon. That would be the perfect time to grab her.

I went by the store and picked up a dreaded wig and some sunglasses so that when I grabbed her, I wouldn't be recognized. While I was following Jojo, I learned where the kids went to camp. The morning I decided to abduct Cassie, I arrived early in hopes that I would catch a glimpse of Celeste when she dropped her off. To my disappointment, it was Kadarius who brought her. One thing I did notice was that their son didn't get out of the car. *This is going to be too easy*, I told myself.

It was about 7:45 in the morning, and the camp was scheduled to let out at 5 o'clock. There was no way I was about to sit out there that long. I had to think of a way to get her out earlier than that. Twelve-thirty was the longest I was willing to wait. That way, at least they would have fed the little brat before I snatched her. I continued to think, and then an idea popped in my head. There was one person that had been itching to help me with this mission.

"Are you busy? I need a favor."

"I'm never too busy for you, baby. What you need?"

I gave her the rundown of what I needed her to do and the information she would need.

"Give me five minutes," she told me.

After what seemed like the longest five minutes ever, she called me back and told me everything was a go. I thanked her and told her I would reward her with something nice later. I waited about fifteen minutes before walking into the camp. I knew I would need my gun, so I made sure it was loaded and on my side. I put on my disguise and went inside.

"Good afternoon. I'm John Spivey. I believe my sister Celeste Norwood called about me picking up my niece Cassie."

"Good afternoon Mr. Spivey. Yes, she called. If you just sign here, we can go get Cassie for you."

I signed the paper then pretended that I had an urgent call to make. I asked if they could have Cassie meet me outside. Thankfully, they agreed. I stepped outside the office. When Cassie walked out, one of the directors was with her. I wasn't expecting that. To play it off, I hugged her and whispered in her ear.

"I have a gun in my pocket, and I'm not afraid to use it. Do as I say, and you won't get hurt."

Cassie nodded her head and told the camp director she would see her later. We went to my car, got in, and I sped off before anybody figured out what I had done.

"Who are you, and why are you doing this?" Cassie cried.

"Don't you recognize me, sweetheart?"

I took off the wig and that so she would see my face.

"Oh my god! How did you find me?"

"Don't worry your pretty little head about that."

"Are you going to kill me?"

"Not if you do as I say."

"Please don't touch me again."

I didn't respond to what she said. The only reason I touched her was to get a rise out of her mother. Cassie didn't need to know that, though. While we were riding, I was trying to think of a place to hold her captive. Thanks to her mother, we couldn't go to the cabin. My house was a no go because it was in the center of everything, and there were too many ways for her to escape. I decided to take Cassie to the person that helped me get her. I called her to let her know I was bringing her something special.

"Is everything okay, baby?" she quizzed as soon as she picked up.

"Everything is perfect. Just wanted you to know that I'm

bringing you a gift."

"Ooh, I love gifts! I'll go out and get what I need for it."

I told her I would let her know when we got closer. I also told her to have a nurse who could look at my wounds because I hadn't been following the care instructions that I had been given. I forgot about her, not knowing that I had been shot and got annoyed when she started asking questions. I told her we would talk more about it when I get there.

I looked in the back seat and noticed Cassie was balled up crying. I started to feel sorry for her but quickly dismissed the thought. Somebody had to pay for her mother's sins. What better person than her daughter.

Chapter 33: Hell Hath No Fury

Kadarius

"Hey Charlotte," I greeted when I answered my phone.

"Kadarius, I went to pick up Cassie, and they said her uncle picked her up."

"Her uncle?"

"Yes, they said Celly called and said that her uncle would be picking her up. Something isn't right."

"I'm on my way up there."

I woke KJ up and told him to come with me. He wasn't feeling well this morning and asked to stay home. Something told me to make Cassie stay home, too, especially after hearing the shit she told me and the shit that was going on with Celeste. The cops still haven't gotten back to me about her whereabouts. I was going to the police station to check on things when Charlotte called me about Cassie.

Celeste didn't have any brothers, and mine didn't live here, so there was no way one of them picked up Cassie. I sped to the camp, threw the car in park, and jumped out with KJ on my tail.

"Hello, Mr. Norwood," the camp director greeted me.

"Yo, drop the formalities and tell me where the fuck my daughter is."

"As I explained to Ms. Myers, Mrs. Norwood called and said that Cassie's uncle would be picking her up."

"And as I explained to you, there is no uncle!" Charlotte replied.

"Exactly! Celeste isn't even available to call up here, so I know she didn't call," I added.

"We had no idea. I'm sorry."

"You can shove that sorry right up your ass!" Charlotte yelled.

"So, you mean to tell me you let a stranger come up here and pick up my daughter? What kind of bullshit operation are you running here?"

"Mr. Norwood, I understand you're upset, but there is no need for the foul language," the director said.

"Bitch, you lucky he's not beating your ass. Instead of you worrying about the type of language he using, you need to be calling the police because my niece has been kidnapped."

Hearing the word kidnapped sent me in rage. I asked what the man looked like. She explained that he had dreads and sunglasses. That pissed me off even more. That clearly was a disguise. She pulled out the log and showed me where he signed Cassie out. The name was just a bunch of scribbled letters. I looked over at KJ, and he was in tears. I hated for him to have to hear this, but I was scared to let him out of my sight.

The director called the police, and when they arrived, I told them everything that was going on. They asked for Cassie's description and what she was wearing so that they could put out an Amber Alert for her. Once that was done, the only thing we could do was wait.

"Mr. Norwood, can you think of anybody who would do this?"

"No, I can't," I lied.

I knew exactly who did this, but I wasn't going to tell the police that. I would handle this son of a bitch myself. Once we were done answering questions, I instructed KJ to go with Charlotte. He was scared, so I had her book them a room in Jersey for the night. Being outside of the city would make him feel better. I promised him that I would find his sister and bring her home safely.

After making sure they were good, I headed to my destination. Once I was there, I used my key to open the door and immediately charged at my target.

"Where the hell is my daughter, you sick son of a bitch?" I yelled at Reggie.

"Why the fuck would I know where your daughter is? Keeping up with your child is not in my job description."

"Somebody pretending to be her uncle took her from camp today. I know it was you. Now, where is she?"

I walked around screaming Cassie's name but got no response. Thinking he had her somewhere tied up with her mouth taped closed, I started tearing that damn condo apart looking for her. When I didn't find her, I went back to Reggie.

"I will ask you one more time, where the fuck is my daughter?"

"And for the last time, I don't know!"

I reached on my side for my gun and realized I had left it. I went into the kitchen, got a knife, and grabbed Reggie.

"You've been threatening my family since you found out I wasn't leaving my wife for you. I know you took her. Now, where is she?"

"I don't have…"

Before he could finish his sentence, I sliced his throat. That wasn't my intention when I picked up the knife, but I got frustrated when he kept lying about not knowing where Cassie was. Looking down at his body, I realized a dead man couldn't give me the answers I needed. For the next few minutes, I walked around the condo, trying to decide what to do. After about twenty minutes, I decided to clean up the blood and get rid of the body. Throwing it in a river was a no go. There were too many witnesses and the possibility of it washing up. While I was cleaning the blood, I came up with the idea to bury Reggie in the backyard of the home Celeste and I once shared.

I went to the store and got some extra-large trash bags, and duct tape then went back and tied up the body. Once it was secured, I went to the police station to find out if there were any leads on Cassie and Celeste. The police had no leads on Cassie and told me that Celeste was somewhere safe. I wondered why she hadn't reached out to me, but I couldn't worry about that. Right now, my daughter was my main concern.

I called Charlotte to check on KJ. She said he was fine and had fallen asleep. I then went back to the condo to wait for nightfall to get rid of the body.

Chapter 34: Final Warning

Celeste

"I'm fine, can you please let me out of here," I said to the nurse, aggravated that they were still holding me here.

I've been in this hospital for two days now. I just wanted to go home and hold both of my kids and stay put until Tykell was found, or better yet found dead. After I found out that he wasn't where I left him, I felt like the world was spinning me around, and I was stuck on a rollercoaster I couldn't get off of.

"After your test results come back, we'll be sure when you'll be able to leave," the nurse informed me, walking out of the room.

I sighed and threw the covers from over my legs, swinging them over the bed. I ran my fingers through my hair, still terrified about what the hell I've been through. My nerves were so bad right now that the simplest shit made me jump. I heard knocking on the door before it opened, revealing Charlotte, Angela, and Laurel. Charlotte looked as if she'd been crying, and I knew me being missing took a toll on her. It took a toll on all of them because I was the youngest. She ran over to me and embraced me into a tight hug as if she didn't want to let me go.

"I'm fine. I'm sorry guys. I would have called you sooner if they would have let me have visitors."

"Celeste, we need to talk," Laurel spoke, sitting on the bed next to me.

"Wassup?"

"First, how are you feeling? Are you okay?"

"I'm fine, but can you do me a favor?"

"Yeah?"

"Can you call Kadarius for me? I've been trying to get in touch with him from left and right. He probably not answering because he don't know the hospital's number. Can you tell him to bring Cassie and KJ over?"

"Celeste, about that. We have to t—"

Laurel was interrupted by a knock on the door and the nurse coming back in the room with a clipboard in her hand.

"Mrs. Norwood, can I talk to you real quickly if you don't mind?" the nurse asked.

"Yeah."

"This is a private matter. I will have to ask your guests to leave. I'm not sure if you want me to tell you this around them or not."

"They are my family. You can tell me."

"Mrs. Norwood, from your charts, everything looks good, but the day you arrived here unconscious, you were hemorrhaging. Were you aware that you were twelve weeks pregnant?"

"What? No," I replied, feeling that tightening sensation in my chest.

Had I known I was pregnant, I wouldn't have been drinking how I was drinking, and I would have taken precautions. Hearing that I miscarried had me confused and saddened at the same time. The thing was the sadness washed away when I realized who I was pregnant by. After Kadarius and I agreed to get divorced, we haven't touched one another since. Tykell was the father of my baby. I swallowed the lump in my throat as everyone gave me worried faces.

"Are you okay, Mrs. Norwood?" the nurse asked.

"Yeah, I just need a minute."

"Take all the time you need." I watched her walk out the door, leaving my sisters here and me to digest the news.

"Celly, I'm sorry to he—"

"I don't wanna talk about it," I interrupted Laurel.

"A miscarriage is something serious. Are you going to tell Kadarius?" Angela quizzed.

"I said I don't want to talk about it. Look, can you call him and tell him to bring my kids to me?"

"Look, I can't tell her. Angela, tell her," Charlotte expressed, walking out the room, wiping her eyes.

"Tell me what?"

"Celly, Cassie was taken from camp this morning."

"What?" I asked in disbelief, feeling my heart drop. That was something a parent never wanted to hear.

"Cassie was kidnapped."

"No, no, she's at camp. Where the fuck is my child?" I yelled, trying to get out of bed.

"Celeste, calm down. Look, the cops are doing what they can."

"I don't give a fuck! Where the hell is my daughter?" I yelled, failing to hold the tears in. Laurel pulled me in her arms, letting me cry on her chest.

The sound of the hospital phone going off interrupted my sobs. Angela answered before looking at me.

"It's for you."

"Look, she can't take it right now," Laurel voiced.

"They said it's important."

I wiped my eyes before taking the phone from Angela.

"I told you not to play with me. Let's see if Cassie knows how to follow directions," Tykell taunted, hanging up in my face.

To Be Continued...